'I decided to look for someone out here. I think you might fit the bill.'

The doctor screwed up his eyes as he scrutinised her intently in the moonlight. She was aware of a rapid increase in her pulse rate. 'Why me?' she stammered.

'Because you're a trained nurse, you speak Malay and English and you've survived the climate for four years.' He was about to add that another thing in her favour was that she was married so, presumably, she wouldn't pose an emotional threat to him or disturb his well-ordered life, but he thought better of it. Best to be totally professional . . .

'Do you have any children?' he asked warily.

A faraway look came into her expressive brown eyes. 'No children,' was her quiet reply.

There was a brightness in her eyes that he couldn't quite discern in the half-light of the moon. He thought for a moment that it was a tear, but she brushed her hand across her face swiftly and he decided he must have been mistaken.

Margaret Barker trained as a State Registered Nurse at a large hospital in the North of England. Soon afterwards, she married a graduate from the nearby university and they have recently celebrated thirty happy years of marriage. They have two sons and a daughter, and one grandchild. Their work has taken them to America, Africa, Asia and Europe, and this has given Margaret ideas for the books which she has set overseas; her own teaching hospital has provided the background for her English stories. She and her husband now live in a sixteenth-century thatched cottage near the sea.

Margaret Barker has written eight other Doctor Nurse Romances, the most recent being *Hong Kong Surgeon*, *Olympic Surgeon* and *Anatomy of Love*.

MONSOON SURGEON

BY
MARGARET BARKER

MILLS & BOON LIMITED
ETON HOUSE 18–24 PARADISE ROAD
RICHMOND SURREY TW9 1SR

First published in Great Britain 1987
by Mills & Boon Limited

© Margaret Barker 1987

Australian copyright 1987
Philippine copyright 1987

ISBN 0 263 75947 4

Set in 11 on 11½ pt Linotron Times
03–1287–48,700

Photoset by Rowland Phototypesetting Limited
Bury St Edmunds, Suffolk
Made and printed in Great Britain by
William Collins Sons & Co Limited, Glasgow

CHAPTER ONE

THE TROPICAL sun beat down mercilessly, but the heavy clouds were laden with the makings of a sudden downpour, as the monsoon wind blew inland over the unsettled, white-capped sea. Anna stared out of the hospital window and shivered in anticipation of the storm, as she watched the willowy casuarina trees along the shore bend low in windblown curves. The fishermen waited by their empty boats, not daring to sail against the force of the mighty monsoon.

The sudden wailing of a child brought her attention back to her patients. She had finished the routine morning work and was waiting to be relieved by one of the other staff nurses before going off duty for the afternoon. Her white cotton uniform was sticking to her damp skin and she was looking forward to a long cool mango juice.

'What is it, little one . . . *sakit apa*?' Anna smiled down into the trusting brown eyes slanting in the thin mahogany face.

The little girl replied in Malay, 'I'm thirsty.'

'Well, that's easily remedied.' Anna held the tiny dark head in one hand and the glass of cold water in the other. 'Not too quickly . . . just a little sip, Hayati.' Until a firm diagnosis had been arrived at, the little patient was on restricted fluids, to prevent a recurrence of her vomiting syndrome. It might be a simple bacterial disorder or it could be something more sinister, thought Anna anxiously.

She settled Hayati back on her pillows and squeezed her hand. Poor little mite! It's a pity there are no relatives to look after her, she worried, as she looked round the ward. Most of the other children had a mother or grandmother in loving attendance. They got in the way sometimes, but it was a blessing to know that the children were happy and secure during their stay, not pining for home or loved ones. The tiny patient closed her eyes wearily.

'That's right—sleep well, Hayati,' whispered Anna.

There was a loud crack of thunder and the heavens opened. She flew to the windows to close them against the driving rain.

'Let me help. Sorry I'm late,' said a breathless voice as a young Chinese staff nurse breezed on to the ward.

The rain was lashing noisily against the panes and the atmosphere was hot and humid by the time they had succeeded in shutting out the storm. Anna glanced up at the fans in the roof, whirring inefficiently in an attempt at making the air more bearable. It's time we had air-conditioning, she thought for the hundredth time that day.

'I'll be back at five,' she told Staff Nurse Wong, as she finished giving her report. 'Keep an eye on Hayati. She's asleep at the moment.'

'I will,' replied the young nurse. 'Have a nice afternoon.' She watched her colleague gathering up her things and wondered, as all the medical staff did, where she was going off to. Anna Gabell is such a dark horse, she thought. Three months she's been with us and nobody knows anything about her—except that she's an exceptionally good nurse, trained in London. But what on earth she's doing out here in this dilapidated place, I can't imagine!

Anna paused as she passed the sign on the ward door, Wad Kanak—Children's Ward, and looked down the row of beds and cots. Although conditions were primitive here, she still enjoyed her work. It was very satisfying. I shall be glad to come back on duty, she thought. She was dreading the long afternoon ahead, as she set off down the corridor towards the Bilek Kecemasan—Casualty Department. A wizened old man, coughing profusely, was sitting beneath a notice that read Dilarang Merotok—No smoking. She was about to remonstrate when Sister Kasim came out of a cubicle and bore down upon the hapless patient.

Through the open door Anna could see the rain bouncing on the driveway, filling the potholes in the worn surface. She started to remove her white staff nurse's cap, with its distinctive blue band denoting rank, allowing her shoulder-length dark brown hair to fall free. Deftly she coiled a length of batik—Malay wax-printed cotton—round her head, put the cap in her shopping bag and opened her umbrella. It was at that moment that she saw Razali, grinning all over his good-natured brown face as he brought his ramshackle old bone-shaker to a halt outside the hospital entrance. He waved to her through his steamed-up window and she waved back, feeling thankful that she wouldn't have to trek across to the car park in the torrential rain. Bending her head against the onslaught, she hurried out to the waiting car. As she crossed the driveway there was a screech of brakes and a waterfall of muddy puddle drenched her white uniform.

'You stupid woman!' cried the irate driver of a large, air-conditioned blue Daimler. 'What the hell do you think you're doing, wandering across the road like that?'

The man had wound down his window only a fraction of an inch so that she could hear his abuse but he would remain dry inside his luxurious limousine. Anna glanced down at the mud on her uniform in fury.

'You've got no right to drive in here so recklessly,' she screamed at the driver's window. 'This is a hospital, not a race-track!'

But the driver had set the vehicle in motion again, the window closing automatically with a smooth whirring action, as he dismissed her as some hysterical relative of a patient, or perhaps a domestic employee with her native headgear. She should have been looking where she was going, he thought angrily as he steered his car towards the car park. Might have been killed!

Anna caught a glimpse of thick brown hair above the arrogant face, but the features were indistinguishable as the car swept away. Seeing the state of her clothes, she was tempted to run after him, but Razali's gentle voice calmed her down.

'Come, Anna,' he called, opening the passenger door with a loud creaking noise and holding out his hand.

She climbed into the stuffy vehicle and flashed Razali a grateful smile. Her brother-in-law never lost his temper. He was always docile, relaxed, a tower of strength—and goodness knows, she had needed to lean on him often enough since she came out to Malaysia four years ago! Through the misty window she could see the hospital gates with the large painted sign, Hospital Daerah Penasing— Government Hospital of Penasing. They narrowly missed an ambulance as it tore through the gates, its red light flashing ominously, lighting up the distinctive red crescent-shaped emblem beside the word Ambulan.

Razali took one hand off the wheel and placed it over hers. 'OK?' he asked, without taking his eyes from the rainsoaked road ahead.

Anna nodded and removed her hand gently, not wanting to hurt his feelings. 'I'm tired,' she murmured as she closed her eyes and tried to get comfortable on the hard seat. What a dreadful car this is, she thought, as one of the loose springs sprang through the ancient upholstery. Must be a collector's item—nearly as bad as mine!

They were driving along Penasing main street with its quaint mixture of Malaysian, Chinese and Indian shops and buildings before Anna broke the silence.

'It was good of you to collect me.' She opened her round brown eyes to study Razali's profile as he gripped the wheel.

'It was nothing. I came to pray,' he answered quietly, without looking at her.

Ah yes, she thought. He's ever the good Moslem, faithful to his father's religion—and his mother's orders! If he stopped going to the mosque for regular prayer, Safiah would make his life a misery. On his day off from work as a builder's clerk, Anna had known him to go five times to the mosque. He was much more devout than her husband had been. The brothers had been different in so many ways; only the physical likeness stamped them as being from the same family. And Ibrahim's university education in England had removed more of his Malaysian heritage. He had been torn between two cultures in the end. The end! She shivered as she remembered that fateful day when the police came to tell her Ibrahim had died, crushed in his car by an out-of-control lorry on the winding road through the jungle. It had been a day like this, strong monsoon winds and stormy rain bouncing off the uneven surface of the road. He hadn't stood a chance in the head-on collision. Her mind had gone blank when they told her, and then, as the confused worries came tumbling back, she had remembered Safiah. 'Dear God! His mother was with him!' she had cried in anguish.

They had reassured her that Safiah would live, as indeed she did, but the crash had taken away the use of her legs. For three years she had been confined to a wheelchair, querulous, exacting and impossible to satisfy.

Anna sighed as the car stopped in front of the family house, its peeling paint reminding her yet again of her constant need to give more financial help. Is there no end to it? she thought as she swung the creaking car door open and stepped carefully over the rust.

The rain was beginning to abate and as the sun peered from behind a cloud a huge rainbow arc reached out from the horizon of the choppy sea. She pulled the length of batik from her head and shook out her hair. Razali glanced sideways and smiled fondly.

'You look much prettier like that,' he said, in a gentle voice.

'Razali!' his mother called from the open door-way where Zaleha, her nursing attendant, had pushed the wheelchair, so that her mistress could await the arrival of her one remaining son. Safiah launched into a tirade in rapid Malay and Anna was only able to grasp the general gist of it; something about a telephone call and an interview for a new job.

Anna smiled to herself. Poor Safiah! She had been so ambitious for her sons, pushing the elder one, Ibrahim, until he won the coveted scholarship. She had put all her eggs in one basked and there was not enough money to educate the younger one. Razali had left school as soon as possible and taken the first available job. From that day, his mother had continually urged him to find something better. From the shrill excitement in her voice it appeared she seemed to have found something suitable at last.

'It will mean living away from home,' the matri-arch was explaining in a rapid dialect which she knew her daughter-in-law found difficult to under-stand. Born in Indonesia, Safiah often reverted to her childhood language if she had anything to conceal. And today she knew that Anna would not be pleased to lose the emotional support of her brother-in-law. It would mean more family responsibility on her shoulders. But the girl is young enough, she thought, without a qualm. Why shouldn't she help to support us? She glanced at the muddy white dress and wrinkled her nose disapprovingly.

'What have you been doing to yourself, girl?' she asked, in Malay.

Anna took a deep breath to dispel her

annoyance, before answering politely, in the same
language, 'A car drove too near me and I got
splashed, Mother.'

'You must go and change at once,' was the stern
reply.

Thankful to escape further scrutiny, Anna ran up
the wooden stairs to her room. It was the room she
had shared for almost a year with Ibrahim. What
memories it brought back! She thought of the first
few idyllic weeks when, being so much in love, she
hadn't cared about the differences in culture, the
lack of money and the constant nagging of her
mother-in-law. Certainly it had been different
from their carefree life together in London, when
Ibrahim had simply moved into her flat near the
university and they had been blissfully happy.
When he got his degree in engineering and asked
her to marry him, she was over the moon. It had
seemed so romantic to fly out to Malaysia to be
married.

But even on her wedding day Safiah had criti-
cised and scolded her, and Anna had found herself
reduced to tears.

'Don't worry, darling,' Ibrahim had told her as
they lay in the carved wooden bed she was now
sitting on. 'I'll make a lot of money and buy us a
house. But I promised my father before he died
that I would look after Mother. And I can't afford
to keep two homes going yet.'

And they had made love, and nothing else
seemed to matter. But after those first honeymoon
weeks, the tension had mounted in the house.
Safiah treated Anna like an unpaid servant, expecting instant obedience. When Anna begged Ibrahim
to let her go back to nursing, he was horrified.

'You're a married woman now,' he had replied, and she had thought how much he had changed since those halcyon student days in London.

They began to argue about money, about her lack of privacy in the house—Safiah would simply barge into their room without knocking, and expect Anna to run some errand for her, or start work immediately in the kitchen—but mostly about what the clash of cultures was doing to their marriage. If Anna had not been so proud, she would have got on a plane and flown back to England. But her mother had warned her it wouldn't work . . .

'Flying off to the other side of the world!' she had taunted, glancing over the top of her pince-nez at her only daughter, who had insisted on interrupting an interesting Bridge afternoon with the appalling news that she was going to marry some foreigner or other. 'Well, you needn't think I'm going to come out to wherever it is you're going. The very idea! English boys not good enough for you, is that it? . . . And your father wouldn't have approved!' she shrieked after her departing daughter as the door of the chintzy drawing room slammed shut. 'It's a good thing Victor isn't here to witness such behaviour,' she added to the embarrassed ladies seated round the card table. 'Now, where were we? Did you say two clubs, Priscilla . . . ?'

So Anna had determined to stick it out for at least a year before going back and picking up the threads of her nursing career again. But she had kept alive the hope that somehow their marriage could be saved. Somehow they might scrape together the money to run two houses. Even a one-roomed rented flat would be better than living under her mother-in-law's thumb, she had pointed out to Ibrahim, but he was adamant that they would only move out when he could afford to maintain two good houses. Anna saw the future lying bleakly ahead of her. She had spent all her own money in the first few weeks of marriage. There was no escape . . .

And then came the crash. She got up off the bed and peeled off the muddied white dress as she remembered the torment of grief and guilt she had experienced. She searched in the wardrobe for a sarong, winding the cool cotton round her. There was a clean uniform at the back of the wardrobe, she noted with relief. But the sarong would be easier to work in during the long afternoon— because she would have to work! There was always a pile of sewing for her to do, or she would have to help Zaleha in the kitchen.

Sometimes she wondered what the nursing attendant did all day. But, remembering her fight to get domestic help in the house so that she could start nursing again, Anna never complained. It took most of her salary to pay for Zaleha and Vera, the part-time *amah*, but it was infinitely preferable to being imprisoned in the house, day after day, and doing all the work herself, as she had done for three long years after the death of Ibrahim.

Razali was talking earnestly, with his mother when she went down, but Zaleha was nowhere to be seen. Probably gone for a siesta now I've arrived, thought Anna resignedly.

'What would you like me to do, Mother?' she asked quietly.

Safiah glanced approvingly at the slim brown figure in the sarong, thinking how she could easily be mistaken for a Malaysian. The girl was integrating well. She had stopped complaining like she used to when she first came out—full of silly ideas about having her own house, the matriarch remembered. But she's learned some sense at last, although she's taken some breaking in . . .

'There are some sheets to be mended,' she announced harshly. Must keep the girl busy. 'You may use my sewing machine,' she added magnanimously.

'*Terima kasih*,' Anna responded dutifully, even though she didn't feel at all like saying thank you. She went first to the kitchen in search of fruit with which to make juice.

In the fridge she found oranges, mangoes and half a pineapple. She put them all into the new machine she had bought for Safiah's birthday, so that she would drink more fruit juice. Her mother-in-law had pronounced it downright extravagance and confined it to the back of the cupboard, but Anna used it. She made up a large jug full of the delicious liquid, tossed in some ice-cubes and settled down to tackle the sewing.

The long, tedious afternoon wore on, the silence broken only by the droning of the cicadas out in the overgrown garden and the rattling of the ancient sewing machine. She glanced at the clock and saw, with relief, that it would soon be time to go back to hospital.

Razali poked his head round the door as if on cue. 'Do you want a lift?' he asked. 'I am going to the mosque. I could take you on to the hosptal.'

'Drop me at the mosque,' she said, jumping up decisively and putting the cover over the hated

sewing machine. 'I'll walk down the hill from there
—the rain's stopped. Where's your mother?'

'She asleep,' he answered.

That's a relief! thought Anna. I'll make a quick
getaway before she wakes up. By the time she had
changed into her clean uniform, Razali was out at
the front of the house exhorting the car to start. The
rain had done nothing for the sparking plugs,
he thought helplessly, as he pulled the starter
lever. After a few seconds the engine spluttered
into life and he smiled happily. If only he could
get this new job he could buy himself a new
car!

Anna climbed in and they shot off back towards
Penasing in a cloud of oil fumes. Razali glanced at
his pretty sister-in-law, thinking how much he
would miss her if he did move.

'Tomorrow I have an interview for a new job,' he
began tentatively.

'So I gathered,' she said in an easy tone.

'Would you mind if I went away?' he asked,
hoping she would say yes.

'Where would you go?' Anna's voice gave
nothing away.

'Singapore . . . Oh, Anna, it's the chance of a
lifetime! I would be employed by day in the office of
a firm of accountants and in the evening I could
study at the British Council. I've always wanted to
further my education.' His breathless tone con-
veyed his excitement.

Anna smiled as she watched his obvious enthusiasm. It made him appear younger than his
twenty-nine years. Although he was only two years
older than she was, his strength of character had
been a continuing source of solace.

'I hope you get the job,' she said sincerely. 'But I shall miss you.'

'Will you?' He was unable to disguise his eagerness. 'But will you be able to take care of Mother?' he added hastily.

'Of course,' she replied tonelessly. I've no choice in the matter, she thought grimly. It's my duty and I'll carry on.

They fell silent as the car groaned its arduous way up the hill to the mosque. The green dome was shining in the late afternoon sun as the ritual sounds of the call to prayer echoed across the hillside.

'You're sure you don't want me to take you on to the hospital?' asked Razali as they reached the mosque.

'No; I'd like to walk.' Anna got out of the car and looked out towards the sea. It was now calm as a millpond, the monsoon winds having subsided as quickly as they came. She could see the islands in the distance; Tawa, with its skyline row of palm trees, and mysterious Desaman, still shrouded in mist. Yes, she wanted to be alone with her thoughts for a while, as she soaked in the beauty of the coastal scenery. It would help to re-charge her batteries, ready for the evening in hospital.

'I'll see you when I get back from Singapore,' said Razali, scanning her face anxiously. 'Wish me luck.'

'Oh, I do,' she smiled.

He came round the front of the car and took hold of her hand as he bent to kiss her cheek. 'Take care of yourself,' he whispered before turning to walk solemnly up the wide stone steps and into the mosque.

Anna watched him disappear, her mind conjuring up an image of the luxurious interior where she had tried to pray when Ibrahim was alive. She remembered learning the new, unfamiliar ritual of washing in the room at the side of the *bilik sembahying*—the prayer room—before walking barefoot over the thick yellow carpet to her place beside Safiah. The women were segregated from the men, and Anna had tried so hard to learn from her mother-in-law. Since Safiah had been confined to a wheelchair, Anna had been spared the ordeal.

She turned away to walk down the hill to the hospital, unaware that her touching goodbye with Razali had been witnessed by an attractive tall man as he climbed into his blue Daimler. He had stared long and hard at the girl in the white dress. As the Malaysian man had got out of his distinctive old car, Simon Sinclair had been undecided about his companion. The girl was about the same size as the apparition in the thunderstorm, but the beautiful long hair changed her appearance completely.

And she's wearing a white dress, he mused. Could it be she's a nurse at the hospital? Oh dear! Not a very good start on my first day. Without her nurse's cap, it's so difficult to tell. As she raised a hand to smooth back her hair, he caught a glimpse of the thick gold wedding ring.

What a dutiful wife! he thought. Accompanying her husband to prayer. As she turned, he gasped. This wasn't a Malay woman. Although the sun had turned her skin a dusky brown, the features were quite definitely European. Perhaps he'd better make amends for drenching her in rainwater.

When the blue Daimler came to a halt beside her, Anna stared at the smiling face of the driver.

What on earth did he want? She recognised the car immediately. There couldn't possibly be two such vehicles like this in Penasing!

'May I give you a lift? I presume you're going to the hospital,' he began, turning off the ignition.

'I prefer to walk,' she said, increasing her pace.

He was not used to being treated like this, but, swallowing his pride, he turned on the engine and pursued her. Once more he drew alongside.

'Look, I really would like to apologise for drenching you like that. It was raining so hard that . . .'

'It doesn't matter,' she snapped, her brown eyes flashing angrily as she turned to face him. 'I had another uniform at home, as you can see.'

He leaned across and pushed open the passenger door. 'Do let me take you back to hospital,' he said smoothly.

'No, thanks. As I said, I prefer to walk . . . and anyway, I don't accept lifts from strangers.' Even supercilious ones in inordinately expensive cars, she added to herself, getting a certain satisfaction from the surprised look on his face.

He thought I'd jump at the chance of a lift in his precious limousine! He's got a nerve! she told herself. She quickened her step and the blue car shot past her down the hill, its driver staring studiously ahead. Anna grinned. That's put him in his place! she thought gleefully, as she breathed in a welcome breeze from the sea.

A couple of fishing boats were putting out to sea, their brightly coloured sails aglow in the sunlight. The palm trees along the shore stood tall and proud in the calm of the early evening. The scene was so different from when she had left it. The rapid changes in the weather were something which Anna still hadn't got used to. But she loved the sea in all its guises. Even when it was grey and turbulent, she liked to watch the foam-flecked waves.

She went in through Casualty, carefully fixing her cap into place. Staff Nurse Wong greeted her happily, when she arrived on the children's ward. Two heads were always better than one, and she had been worrying about Hayati. Perhaps she should have called in a second opinion during the afternoon, she thought anxiously, but now that Nurse Gabell was here she would know what to do.

'You say her temperature is raised?' queried Anna, instantly on the alert.

'Yes, it's about 37.7.'

'You've notified Dr Singh, I hope?'

'Well, no, because I was waiting to see what you thought.'

Anna drew in a ragged, impatient breath, as she went down the ward to examine the little patient. There was no doubt about it, Hayati was in the grip of a high fever. But there was something else, which had been absent before. The tiny seven-year-old was lying on her back with her knees flexed up to her chin, in obvious pain.

'Where does it hurt, Hayati?' she asked in Malay, as she palpated the abdomen.

The little patient winced as Anna's fingers pressed on the right iliac fossa. There was no need for words: all the signs and symptoms of appendicitis were present. She made the girl as comfortable as she could before ringing for the doctor on duty. As she returned from the phone, she found herself praying that he wouldn't be long. Wheels had to be set in motion quickly if the child was to be saved. There was no operating theatre at Penasing and even minor operations had to be taken miles along the jungle road to the district hospital. It's all so frustrating, Anna thought, remembering all the talk about the need for a surgical unit.

She heard an authoritative step in the open doorway and turned anxiously. But it wasn't Dr Singh, the gentle Indian doctor, as she had expected. Instead, the arrogant features of the tall stranger stared down at her. But this time he wasn't smiling.

'I'm told you have a possible case of appendicitis, Staff Nurse. May I ask who made this diagnosis?' Deep blue eyes stared at her as she made her reply.

'I did.' Her voice was shaking with apprehension. The white coat, open at the front to reveal his expensive silk shirt, and the stethoscope slung casually round his suntanned neck removed what was left of her self-confidence. If only she'd known he was a doctor!

'On what did you base your diagnosis, nurse?' His tone was cold and utterly professional. He was not concerned about her in the slightest—only about the patient.

'Hayati was admitted with generalised abdominal pain which has now localised in the right iliac fossa. She has a recent history of vomiting and her temperature is now 37.7.' The words came out in a breathless rush.

'Age?' he snapped.

'She's seven.'

'We'd better take a look,' he said, moving quickly down the ward.

Anna tried to catch up with him, but his long strides were too much for her.

'This is Hayati, yes?' He turned at the bedside to wait for her.

She nodded as she went to the little girl's side. Hayati reached out a tiny hand and Anna grasped it. 'It's all right, darling. The nice doctor has come to take a look at your tummy,' she whispered soothingly, as she lifted back the cotton sheet.

The doctor's face relaxed as he examined his tiny patient. He spoke gently in Malay and listened attentively to the child's reply. His expert fingers touched the offending area and, noting the obvious pain, released their pressure. He began to explain to the little girl that he was going to make her better, but he would have to put her to sleep for a little while.

Hayati gave the ghost of a smile, thinking what a kind face the nice doctor had. She hoped he really would be able to make her better, because she was tired of being sick and she wanted to go home to help her mummy again. It was tough being the eldest of five children when you were only seven yourself, but she knew her mother depended on her to help with the new baby . . .

Anna longed to interrupt the new doctor. Surely he must know that there was no surgical unit here? The only thing they could do was get Hayati into an ambulance as soon as possible. But it would only upset the little patient if she broke the news in front of her. She waited until he straightened up and turned to leave the bedside.

'There's something I must point out, sir,' she began as they walked back down the ward, her shaky voice betraying her nervousness. 'We have no surgical unit here. Our standard procedure is to despatch the patients to the district hospital at Kedang. They return here for post-operative care . . .'

'All supposing they've survived the journey through the jungle, you mean!' he rapped out harshly. 'It's absolutely archaic to carry on with such an outdated practice!'

'But we have no alternative, sir!' Her voice rose shrilly as she turned to face him, her brown eyes glinting with frustration.

'Correction; you *had* no alternative,' he replied smoothly, a faint smile beginning at the corners of his mouth. 'This is why I'm here—to open up a surgical unit.'

'But we have no operating theatre . . .'

'Stop being so negative!' he snapped. 'There's a perfectly good theatre in the annexe, as I recall. They used it in my father's day . . . simply fallen into disrepair. Where's the phone?'

'Over here, sir.'

He strode past her and the next minute she heard him issuing precise orders in fluent Malay.

'. . . and I want it ready in one hour, Sister!' he finished off.

He's asking the impossible, Anna thought helplessly. She had seen the unused theatre next to the room where they sterilised the dressings in the ancient autoclave. What did he mean, 'in my father's day'?

'I want you to prepare our patient for theatre, Staff Nurse. I presume you can do that?' He towered above her, his confident blue eyes boring inside her.

'Of course, sir.' There was no point in arguing

with an egomaniac like this, she thought grimly.
Just get off my back and leave me to look after my
patients.

'Have you had any theatre experience, Nurse?'

'I was a theatre staff nurse in the UK before . . .
er . . . before my marriage,' she faltered.

'I see. Then perhaps you would assist me with
this case.' He was smiling at her encouragingly,
sensing her nervousness.

For the first time that day, Anna noticed how
handsome he was. The strong, arrogant face would
have appealed to her, back in the days when she
took an interest in the opposite sex. She was instantly appalled at her thoughts and dismissed them
firmly.

'Are you asking or ordering me, sir?' Her voice
was cold and professional as she raised her eyes to
his.

The smile vanished from his lips. 'I would prefer
to think it was your choice. Conscripted staff are no
good to me.'

'I'll assist you if Nurse Wong can cope without
me,' she answered blandly, stung by the con-
temptuous tone of his voice.

'Good. We shall be ready in an hour.' He swung
out of the ward.

Anna went into the sterilising room in search of a
hypodermic syringe. As she drew up the pre-med
she found, uncharacteristically, that her hands
were trembling. The new doctor had affected her
more than she cared to admit.

Hayati took no notice of the tiny pinprick in her
arm. It was nothing compared with the overall
discomfort she was feeling. She stared beseechingly
up at her favourite nurse.

'What's going to happen to me?' she asked weakly.

Anna sat down on the bed and took the little patient's hand in her own as she explained, as simply as possible, about the operation. Hayati's slanting eyelids began to droop as the drug took effect. Anna smoothed back the damp black hair from the little girl's forehead and stood up.

'Don't worry, little one,' she whispered.

Nurse Wong came across the ward from the medicine trolley to quiz her about the new doctor.

'I heard he was coming back,' said the Chinese nurse.

'Back? Where's he been?' Anna asked, trying not to sound too interested.

'England, of course. Where all the top people go for their education—when they can afford it. Then they come back here throwing their weight around. His father was our Resident.'

'Resident?' queried Anna.

'Resident adviser to the Sultan—before Independence, that is. He still lives in the big house on the top of the hill—near the mosque; you must have seen it when you were up there.'

'Not that great palace of a place?' So that was why he was driving down the hill, she thought. He'd been to see his father. She remembered his words, 'in my father's day'. It was all falling into place.

'The very same.' Nurse Wong was warming to her subject. 'I went there once as a child. The Sinclairs were giving a charity garden party and we were all invited. It was lovely!'

'Can you cope while I'm down in theatre?' Anna brought the conversation quickly back to their work.

'Of course I can. I wish I'd been asked to assist. Some people get all the luck!'

Anna wasn't so sure.

CHAPTER TWO

HE WAS waiting for her in the theatre anteroom, tapping his fingers impatiently on the white sheet covering the couch.

'Come along, Staff Nurse; we haven't got all day. I might as well have driven her to Kedang myself in the time it's taken to get this show on the road. At least they would have had some modern equipment.'

Anna was amazed at the transformation that had taken place in the hour since she had seen the irascible Simon Sinclair. He certainly knew how to get things moving! Old dust sheets had been taken off, antique equipment had been sterilised and floors had been scrubbed. Sister Kasim, her face a dusky red from all the exertion, was moving noiselessly round the hastily improvised theatre, setting out instruments and checking that everything was ready for the great man. She had been warned that he would be impatient to start up his new surgical unit, but this was impossible!

He was smiling down at his little patient, speaking in her own language. She gave a wan, drowsy smile in return and closed her eyes, wishing it was all over.

'Where's that anaesthetist?' he muttered. 'Fetch the thiopentone sodium and an ampoule of sterile distilled water, Staff Nurse.'

For an instant, his terminology threw her.

27

'Pentothal, dear,' he explained—unnecessarily, because she had already remembered.

Don't patronise me, she thought, her eyes glinting angrily as she brought over the two ampoules for the surgeon to check. He nodded impatiently before turning his attention on Dr Singh, who had just arrived from Casualty pushing the heavy anaesthetic machine.

'How kind of you to drop in. We were about to begin without you, doctor.'

'I'm sorry to delay you, Mr Sinclair,' began the Indian doctor.

'I shall be known as *Dr* Sinclair out here,' the surgeon announced abruptly. 'It would be too confusing for the patients if they couldn't call me *doktor*, especially when I start up medical services in the offshore islands. When I return to the UK I shall revert to my original title.'

And the sooner the better! thought Anna. This is one human whirlwind we can do without in Penasing. Simon Sinclair is definitely a fish out of water here. Probably has a lucrative private practice in London and decided to do a bit of charity work to salve his conscience . . .

'You'd better go and scrub up, Staff Nurse,' the surgeon snapped. 'By the way, what's your name?' he called after her as she hurried away.

'Nurse Gabell, sir.' She turned to meet his puzzled look.

'Gabell? Is that your maiden name?'

'Yes, sir.' For a moment their eyes met and she experienced a weird shivering feeling down her spine. She noticed the wide-open, deep-set blue eyes showed a glimmer of interest in her as a woman. His lips parted briefly to give a glimpse of strong white teeth, contrasting with the suntanned skin covering his firm, aristocratic features.

'Have you been out here long. Nurse Gabell?' he asked, his tone softening.

'Four years, sir.'

He looked surprised. 'You've survived very well. You look in remarkably good shape.'

To her annoyance she blushed and, turning away quickly, she hurried off to scrub up. What an arrogant creature! she thought as she splashed the water into the basin. Thinks he owns the place! Her hands were trembling as she scrubbed. It was infuriating to think that a mere man could have this effect on her. She turned off the water with her elbow, holding her dripping hands in front of her as she went across to the sterilising room in search of a gown, cap and mask.

When she entered the theatre, everyone was assembled. With a movement of his finger the surgeon indicated her place across the table from Sister Kasim. She was glad she was to be number two in the hierarchy.

'Scalpel, Sister,' he barked.

Anna watched as the skilful hands made a gridiron incision about seven centimetres long, starting just above the level of the anterior superior iliac spine. She reached across to swab the trickle of blood as the lower tissue was exposed, noticing the deep absorption in the blue eyes above the surgeon's mask. He was utterly intent on his task.

'There's the problem!' He had been silent for several minutes, as he probed the tiny abdominal cavity. 'There's an obstruction at the lumen of the appendix cutting off the blood supply from the ileocolic artery. Another few hours and gangrene would have set in and then perforation. I think we've caught it just in time. Phew, it's hot in here!' He glanced despairingly at the ineffective fan above his head.

It was the first time he had shown that he was human like the rest of them, Anna thought as she wiped his sweating brow.

'Thank you, Nurse,' he muttered absently, his eyes glued to the site of operation. 'I'm going to remove the swollen appendix. Fortunately, there are no adhesions . . .'

He worked steadily until the offending organ had been removed and they had reached the suture stage. As the wound closed up neatly, he turned to survey his small team.

'Not bad for a first attempt,' he condescended. 'But remember next time, speed is of the essence when a patient's life is at stake. You can take over Dr Singh. She looks a good colour.'

And with that he swept out of the theatre, pulling off his mask with one hand and his cap with the other.

'Nurse Gabell,' he called over his shoulder, 'come and help me with this damn gown.'

'Yes, sir.' Anna's legs felt weak as she crossed the room. She decided it must be the effect of standing for so long in one position. It couldn't be anything else.

He was standing in the ante-room with his back towards her like a child waiting to be undressed. She seemed to be all thumbs as she fiddled with the ties at the back of his gown. As she released the last one he swung round to face her.

'Thanks.' He tossed the gown in the general direction of the laundry bin. It fell inches from its destination and Anna moved automatically to retrieve it.

'Wait!' His hand was on her arm, fingers closing round the bare flesh. 'Someone else can do that. I want to talk to you.'

'Now?' She was startled by the gentleness of his voice. What could he possibly want to talk about?

'Yes, now. I've got a proposition to make.' He smiled down at her, the corner of his eyes crinkling disarmingly. 'Don't look so worried—I'm not going to compromise you.'

'But what about my patient?' She glanced towards the theatre, her heart beating wildly at being left alone with this disturbing man.

'She's in good hands. There's nothing you can do until she's fully recovered from the anaesthetic. Dr Singh will call you when you're needed. Come outside for a breath of air.' He pushed open the doors to the verandah and strode through them, breathing deeply. 'Ah, that's better! I thought I'd be asphyxiated in that dreadful little theatre. How do you stand it?' he asked as she joined him.

Anna couldn't think of a suitable reply, but it was a rhetorical question anyway. He sank down into the depths of a bamboo armchair, pushing the damp hair from his forehead. 'I'd forgotten how hot it was.'

'Would you like a drink, sir?' she asked impulsively. He really did look whacked, and it was the least she could do.

'How very perceptive of you—and don't call me "sir" when we're relaxing together. My name's Simon,' he said quickly.

Anna gave a dutiful smile as she went off to the little kitchen at the end of the theatre corridor. You may be relaxing, but I feel decidedly tense, she thought anxiously. The sooner she heard the nature of this proposition the better!

The ice in the long, cold mango juice tinkled merrily as she handed him a glass.

He patted the bamboo seat beside him. 'Come and join me.'

It was most definitely an order. Anna put her glass on a low wicker table and peeled off her green theatre gown, rolling it into a damp ball ready for the laundry. The white dress beneath it was crumpled and sticky. She pulled off her theatre cap and the long hair cascaded on to her shoulders. It made her somehow feel very vulnerable to be sitting at such close proximity.

'That's better,' he remarked, reaching out to touch the ends of her hair.

She moved her head and half rose in her seat. 'I'd better get my cap.'

'No, leave it like that until you go back to the ward.' He was smiling, and the blue eyes held a hint of masculine interest.

'About this proposition—' she began hastily, looking out across the hospital gardens.

They had missed the brief twilight while they operated and the bright moon had risen over the sea, casting eerie shadows over the fan-shaped palm trees by the hospital gate. Above them, on the roof of the verandah, a lizard was screeching noisily to its mate.

Simon Sinclair looked upwards, deliberately taking his time. 'Beats me how such a small creature can make so much noise . . . Ah yes, where were we? As you may or may not know, I've come out here to establish a surgical unit, and also to set up medical care for the offshore islands. I'm on a government contract, but I can use my own discretion about the appointment of staff. Before I left London, I tried to find a suitable trained nurse to help me in the second part of my contract. None of the applicants I interviewed was satisfactory, so I decided to look for someone out here. I think you might fit the bill.'

He screwed up his eyes as he scrutinised her intently in the moonlight.

She was aware of a rapid increase in her pulse rate. 'Why me?' she stammered.

'Because you're a trained nurse, you speak Malay and English and you've survived the climate for four years.' He was about to add that another thing in her favour was that she was married so, presumably, she wouldn't pose an emotional threat to him or disturb his well-ordered life, but he thought better of it. Best to be totally professional. 'Anyway, *you* should be telling me all about your good points and *I* should be doing the interviewing.'

She gasped. 'I suppose it hadn't occurred to you that I may not want your precious job,' she snapped.

'Oh, but I think you will, when I outline the favourable terms,' he replied easily. 'It will mean a good increase in salary, for a start.' He was watching her reaction as he said this, thinking all the time about the dilapidated car her husband drove. They must be short of money, he had figured.

'Money isn't everything,' she began, but even as she said it, she knew it would be a great help. She could get someone in to paint the family house and save up for a new fridge to replace the antique model that smelled so awful when you opened the door . . .

'It might entail longer hours,' he continued carefully. Better not let her get carried away. She looks interested, but she may have commitments . . . children perhaps? he wondered.

'I thought there'd be a catch in it.' Anna smiled up at him and he thought how much prettier she was when she relaxed. Yes, she would be a definite asset on his medical travels . . .

'Do you have any children?' he asked warily.

A faraway look came into her expressive brown eyes. 'No children,' was her quiet reply.

There was a brightness in her eyes that he couldn't quite discern in the half-light of the moon. He thought for a moment that it was a tear, but she brushed her hand across her face swiftly and he decided he must have been mistaken.

'So your domestic arrangements are such that you could travel to the islands with me and, in an emergency, spend a night away from home,' he concluded rapidly.

Anna paused before answering. Her mother-in-law would certainly object, but Zaleha was perfectly capable of coping alone. She could give her some extra money to keep her happy, and it would be nice to get away from Penasing occasionally. It was ages since she'd done any travelling. 'I have adequate domestic help . . . It would be possible for me to travel—but I wouldn't like to spend more than one night away from home,' she specified anxiously.

'Perfectly understandable.' Simon smiled at her, thinking that if she were his wife he wouldn't want her to be away from home either. She obviously had an understanding husband, but he would try to ensure that overnight stops were kept to a minimum, for more reasons than the obvious one. 'So we've reached an agreement; that's good.' He held out his hand.

She reached out her own and they shook hands solemnly. As his fingers closed round hers, she felt a delicious tingling sensation shooting up her arm. It was so long since a man had excited her like this. When Razali kissed her cheek, as a dutiful brother-in-law, it had not the slightest effect on her sensations. But this was something different. She would have to be careful . . .

'I'll go and see if Hayati is conscious,' she said, hastily removing her hand as she stood up.

'We'll go together.' There was a decisive ring to his voice. He was already two paces ahead of her. 'I'll make the arrangements about your increase in salary,' he added nonchalantly, as he stepped back into the hospital.

'Thank you.' She followed him inside, thinking he would never know how timely this extra money was. People who are born with a silver spoon in their mouths have no insight in such mundane matters . . .

They found their little patient on the verge of consciousness.

'You can remove the endotracheal tube, nurse.' He was once again the efficient surgeon.

As Anna took the tube from Hayati's mouth, the little girl stirred and opened her eyes.

'When are you going to do the operation?' she asked, in a weak voice.

The surgeon and the staff nurse smiled. This happened so often in hospital. When a patient came round from the anaesthetic, they often didn't realise how long they had been asleep.

Simon Sinclair reached out his hand and took the tiny one in his own. 'We've finished, Hayati,' he said softly, and Anna marvelled at the way he could switch on the bedside manner. He was like two different people—one, impatient and exacting, the other, calm and considerate.

He pulled back the sheet to check the wound, nodding his head approvingly. 'That's fine.'

Anna was checking the tiny pulse.

'Better keep a half-hourly check on TPR and blood pressure,' he advised. 'You can take her back to the ward now. I'll be along later.'

As she returned to the ward with her patient, she found herself wishing she could stay on longer, so that she would see him again. This is ridiculous! she told herself firmly. I'm behaving like a schoolgirl with a crush on the sports master! Just because he's physically attractive it doesn't mean I have to fall for him. Quite the reverse. There were definite reasons why she must never allow herself to fall in love again.

The ward was quiet when the night nurse appeared to take charge. Anna gave her report, urging special attention for her little post-operative patient. As she reached the ward door on her way out, she paused and smiled at the unusual scene. Well, it would be unusual in England to see all these mothers still here, she thought, as she watched the loving care of the faithful Malay women. One was actually curled up in the cot with her baby, while another was preparing to lie down on the floor beside her child's bed. She lingered for a moment, not wanting to admit that it would be nice to catch a glimpse of Simon Sinclair . . . but only because she dreaded the prospect of returning home . . .

In fact, she didn't see him again for a whole week. Dr Singh came into the ward next morning to examine Hayati and quietly explained that his colleague had flown off to do a tour of the islands, assessing the various medical requirements. Anna bit back her disappointment that he hadn't taken her. Anyway, she hadn't had time to explain the new situation to her mother-in-law. She would have to choose the right moment, and she was dreading it.

By the time Dr Sinclair did return, she had managed to convince the old matriarch that the house would not fall down about their heads if Zaleha was left in charge occasionally. The promise of extra money had pleased both of the older women.

He arrived, unannounced, in the middle of a busy morning, carrying a small baby in his arms. He was wearing crumpled white cotton slacks and a short-sleeved shirt, open down the front almost to his leather belt. Sweat was pouring down his face as he deposited his patient on an empty cot.

'Nurse Gabell!'

Anna turned in surprise at the sound of the rich deep masculine voice and was unable to prevent a smile of welcome spreading over her face. The day would certainly become more interesting now he was back!

'Yes, sir?' She hurried across the ward and looked down at the tiny patient.

'I've brought this little one in from Desaman. I suspect we may have a thoracic sarcoma on our hands.' He was gently removing the small cotton shift from the baby.

Anna drew in her breath in dismay as she noted the unnatural bony protuberance in the centre of the chest.

'Magdi is nine months old, although you wouldn't think it to look at him. I found him being cared for by his old grandmother—his mother died when he was born. The old lady asked me if I thought there was anything wrong with him. Apparently she'd noticed how thin he was getting, but not his misshapen thorax. When I pointed it out, she said that a *doktor* had told her all babies had their own distinctive shape! Can you believe it? I think she was rambling, the poor old dear.' He ran a hand through his thick dark hair, in exasperation.

The baby gave a weak cry and lifted his hand to his mouth and started to suck.

'You'd better feed him,' he said abruptly. 'And then we'll take him down to the National University Hospital in Singapore.'

'Singapore?' queried Anna. Her thoughts were in turmoil.

'You did say you would be able to work on my islands project, didn't you, Nurse Gabell?' His blue eyes narrowed ominously.

'Yes, but I thought I'd get a little more warning than this,' she blurted out. 'I mean, I've got arrangements to make . . .'

'If you don't want the job . . .'

'Oh, but I do!' she broke in hastily, then added, with a calmness she didn't feel, 'When would you like me to be ready?'

'As soon as you can. Feed Magdi first—he can only take fluids from a feeding bottle, and no one has ever attempted solids, as far as I can gather. I've arranged for him to have a body scan in the diagnostic department at the National University Hospital this afternoon. I'll call back for you in about an hour—and please be ready!'

He disappeared, as quickly as he had arrived, giving Anna the impression that a monsoon wind had torn through the ward, disrupting the well-ordered routine.

She made up a milk feed and picked up the tiny scrap of a baby. He opened his slanting eyes and stared at her wistfully, as he began to suck gently.

'Come on, Magdi,' she whispered. 'We've got a long journey ahead of us.'

Her mind was flying around all the things she would have to do before setting off. She would ring home and tell them—that would be the hardest part!

When the baby was satisfied, she changed his nappy, using the emergency supply of disposables and packing several into her medical bag. Then she settled Magdi in his cot while she went off to get ready, leaving Nurse Wong in charge. The Chinese nurse was green with envy.

'Nothing exciting ever happens to me,' she said, with a big sigh. 'How long will you be away?'

'I've no idea,' Anna replied breathlessly. 'It depends what time we have the scan. Tonight or tomorrow, I suppose. Look, I must dash . . .'

She escaped before any more questions were asked. Her heart was pounding madly. Steady on! she told herself as she rang home. You'll be exhausted before you reach Singapore.

'Is that you, Zaleha?' She took a deep breath before launching into an account of the emergency.

Zaleha explained that her mistress was still in bed. Would she like her to be brought to the phone?

'Oh no,' Anna replied quickly. 'Just tell her what's happening, and take great care of her in my absence. I'll return as soon as I can.'

She put the phone down, relieved that it had gone so well. Zaleha would cope; she was sure of it. She hurried into the changing room and opened her locker. The interior displayed only one mufti outfit, a cotton skirt and matching blouse in bright pink. She must have been mad to choose that colour! It did nothing for her except make her feel hot, but it would have to do. Anyway, if we return this evening I shan't need it . . . she thought.

She returned to the ward and waited beside the sleeping baby. As she looked down at the tiny wrinkled face she felt a tear pricking behind her eyelid. She reached a hand hastily to her eyes, brushing across them as she always did if she felt broody. She had never allowed herself to mourn the loss of her own baby. He had been very real to her, even though she was only three months pregnant when she miscarried. The obstetrician at Kedang Hospital had told her she mustn't get pregnant again—something about a narrow pelvis, she remembered. But she never had gone into it thoroughly, because Ibrahim had been killed that day and there didn't seem much point . . .

'Ready?' Simon Sinclair's deep voice interrupted her thoughts.

She gave him a bright smile as she reached down for the sleeping baby.

'Yes, I'm ready.'

CHAPTER THREE

THE BLUE Daimler carved its way through the
jungle. Anna was glad that Simon had dispensed
with the suggested *ambulan*. This was a much more
comfortable way to travel. She held the baby close
to her as the car bounced over the monsoon
potholes. He had been fractious at the start of the
journey, so she had lifted him out of his carry-cot
and soothed him off to sleep. It seemed a pity to
disturb him when the road was so rough. She
watched the firm hands on the wheel; typical
surgeon's hands, she thought—sensitive, fine-
boned and immaculately manicured. The golden
hairs on the back of the hands contrasted sharply
with the dark, suntanned skin.

'Everything OK back there?' he asked suddenly,
without taking his eyes off the road.

'Fine, thanks. He's asleep again.' They hadn't
spoken for at least half an hour and her voice
croaked with the dryness of her parched throat.

'You've got a way with babies; should have some
of your own—but wait until I've got the islands
project going!'

She was sitting directly behind him and could see
that he was smiling, in the driving mirror, watching
her reaction.

'Don't worry,' she muttered, through clenched
teeth, 'I won't let you down.' She had never been
able to discuss the problem with anyone and she
certainly wasn't going to unburden herself here on

the jungle road to a rich doctor who thought only
patients could suffer. She leaned back against the
luxurious leather upholstery. It smelled new—
can't be more than a few weeks old, she figured.
He must have bought it to impress the staff at
Penasing . . .

She closed her eyes and allowed herself to be
rocked to and fro by the motion of the limousine.
The air-conditioning was such bliss after the cruel
heat of the midday sun. I mustn't fall asleep, she
told herself; not when I'm on duty. She half opened
her eyes and saw that they were going through a
rubber plantation. The road had improved slightly.
Now she caught a glimpse of a few tin shacks, some
tables out at the front and a group of Malays,
drinking in the shade. I'd love a cool drink, was her
last thought before she drifted off to sleep.

She awoke with a jerk as they were approaching
the causeway at Johore Bahru. The sleeping baby
was still clutched in her arms. She glanced at the
sardonic face in the driving mirror.

'Sleep well?' he asked, a hint of sarcasm in his
deep voice.

'Where are we?' Anna was annoyed that he had
caught her off guard.

'Just about to go through the immigration check.
Have you got your passport handy?'

She fiddled in her bag, trying not to wake Magdi,
but the movement disturbed him and he started to
cry.

'Come on, nurse; put the baby down, for
heaven's sake!'

Stung by the irritation in his voice, she obeyed,
and the tiny scrap bawled even louder. The Malay
official stared out of his little box, wondering why

the man in the Daimler was getting so impatient.
He didn't mind waiting . . .

When eventually the passport was produced,
Simon Sinclair's face was a mask of thunder. 'You
could have had it ready,' he muttered under his
breath. 'It's the only thing you've had to do for the
past couple of hours.'

Magdi was bawling his head off now, and the hot
air seeping through the open window was doing
nothing for Simon's temper.

'Can't you keep that baby quiet?' he snapped in
desperation. 'What's the good of bringing a nurse
with me if she spends half her time napping!'

Anna didn't trust herself to reply. She snuggled
the baby against her and he stopped crying as they
crossed the causeway to Singapore. 'See the pretty
skyscrapers over the water,' she whispered to
Magdi. Even Dr Sinclair's wrath couldn't dispel her
excitement as she looked out at the blue water on
either side of the man-made causeway.

Cars were streaking past on the other side of the
road, going from Singapore to Malaysia, and then
they reached Immigration. The surgeon had re-
tained her passport, so this time there was no delay.
They were in Singapore.

Strange that I've only been here twice in the four
years I've been out here, Anna thought. The first
time she had only seen the inside of the airport
before the long trek to Penasing and her new life.
She shivered as she remembered how she had been
full of hope and anticipation, ready to make a
success of their marriage. If only she'd known what
lay in store for her, she would have taken the next
plane back! And the second time, she remembered, was when Ibrahim had a business trip. He

had taken her with him. It was to have been a sort of second honeymoon, an attempt to patch up their marriage. But they had quarrelled—and then made it up. She smiled to herself; she had often wondered if their baby had been conceived that night in the poky little hotel just off the Serangoon Road . . .

'Do you like Singapore?' Simon Sinclair's deep voice brought her back to the present with a jolt.

'I've only been here a couple of times.'

'You should come here more often,' he said expansively. 'It's a wonderful place—one of my favourite cities. I don't know which I prefer, Hong Kong or Singapore.'

Anna remained silent, thinking that the surgeon's life-style was light years removed from her own. Magdi was sound asleep again, so she dared to return him gently to his cot on the back seat. They were driving through the city to the outer suburbs.

'There's the National University Hospital,' Dr Sinclair pointed out.

She had a first impression of a shining white complex of ultra-modern buildings. It looked like something for the twenty-first century. Nor was her impression dispelled as they went inside. Wide glass doors opened automatically to welcome them into the spacious, air-conditioned interior. A junior radiographer was waiting in the well-planned foyer, briefed to approach the great man as soon as he arrived.

'Dr Sinclair?' the young man asked deferentially. 'I've been asked to take you straight to our diagnostic department.'

'Good. Lead the way.' As always, the surgeon

was impatient to get started. He glanced approvingly at the efficient equipment on either side of the long corridor leading to Diagnostics. If only he could transplant half this efficiency to Penasing . . .

The baby was awake but strangely quiet as Anna carried him, two steps behind the doctor. It's almost as if he too is overawed by the place, she thought.

A senior radiographer showed her where to lay her patient on a wide couch. 'When did he have his last feed?' he asked.

'Four hours ago.'

'Fine, we can give him a general anaesthetic. It will be much easier,' the radiographer said.

It was a matter of minutes before the baby was under the body scan and Anna and the surgeon were watching the viewing screen. The unnatural tumour showed up vividly.

Simon Sinclair drew in a ragged breath. 'It looks like a scirrhous sarcoma,' he whispered to Anna. 'But we shan't know until we can ascertain the histology and that, of course, will mean surgery. Ralph James is standing by.'

Anna recognised the name of one of Singapore's top surgeons. Sinclair certainly knows how to get things moving, she thought. I wonder who's paying for all this. It can't be the dear little patient's granny on Desaman! She knew that the three-tier system of medical expenses in Singapore had no provision for penniless uninsured patients from Malaysia.

A tall, distinguished man with a small tufted grey beard had joined the group around the video screen. Simon Sinclair stood up and the two men shook hands.

'Good to see you again,' they were both saying

quietly as their eyes strayed back to the picture of the tumour.

'How soon before you could operate?' Simon Sinclair was displaying his customary impatience.

'I'm at your disposal for the next few hours, Simon,' said the older man. 'I've cleared the decks for the day, so I can operate at once. The sooner the better, I'd say, from the look of things. We don't want to get secondaries in the lungs.'

'Do you want me to assist, Ralph?'

'No need, old chap. I've got a competent team and besides, too many cooks and all that . . .' He raised a hand to stroke his beard thoughtfully, already considering the best approach to the imminent surgery. There was not a second to lose.

Anna glanced at Simon Sinclair's face, sensing his disappointment at not being included. It would be like having two prima donnas in the same opera, she thought wickedly. She looked through the inner window at her tiny, motionless patient, sad to be leaving him but knowing that he was in good hands. This must surely be one of the most advanced hospitals in the world, was her reassuring conclusion.

An hour later they left the streamlined hospital and, surgeon and nurse, stood outside in the late afternoon sunshine. The last hour had been a revelation to Anna, who had been taken on a guided tour of the hospital by the young radiographer who had first met them. It had to be curtailed because of the time factor. She didn't want to keep Simon Sinclair waiting when he had specified the exact minute they were to meet!

'Did you enjoy your tour?' he asked, screwing up his eyes to avoid the glare of the sun.

'Very much. Oh, if only we had half the equipment at Penasing!'

'Just what I was thinking.' He put a hand under her elbow and steered her towards his car. 'I saw Magdi into theatre. Let's hope we've caught it in time,' he said earnestly as he unlocked the car door.

She climbed in beside him, feeling the intense heat of the closed-up vehicle sap at her flagging strength. 'When shall we know the outcome?' she asked.

'Ralph said to ring him later this evening.' He had turned on the ignition and was fiddling with the air-conditioning. 'They offered us accommodation at the hospital, by the way, but I said we'd find something in town. We may as well see something of Singapore while we're here.'

Anna's heart thumped rapidly as the car purred quietly out of the hospital car park. The thought of a night in Singapore with this devastating man made her feel quite faint. And she had absolutely nothing to wear—except the awful pink skirt and blouse!

'What we need is a breath of air,' Simon announced as he headed away from the hospital. He glanced at the slim figure in the white dress beside him. 'Take that wretched cap off, girl, and try to relax. We're off duty now. Would you like to see the Botanic Gardens?'

'Oh yes' she enthused spontaneously, forgetting her worries about what she should wear for an instant. 'But what about my uniform dress?'

'It's simply a pretty little white dress—perfectly suitable for a stroll in the park. Stop fussing.'

She kept quiet during the rest of the drive, allowing him to concentrate on his manoeuvres through the dense traffic. It was the peak of the rush hour in Singapore and everyone was hell-bent on getting home. Eventually he pulled up outside the iron gates in Napier Road, and Anna breathed a sigh of relief. It would be good to stretch her legs after being cooped up all day.

As she stepped out of the car and walked through the ornate gates, the beauty of the landscaped parklands and sweeping lawns took her breath away. Tall, regal palms stretched upwards towards the darkening sky.

'It's beautiful,' she breathed as she quickened her pace, oblivious to the fact that Simon was still locking up the car. For once, she was ahead of him!

'Hey, wait for me!' he called boyishly, and she turned at the sound of his carefree voice.

He was sprinting towards her with long, athletic strides. She caught in her breath as she thought how physically desirable he looked. Yes, desirable . . . she had to admit it. It was a long time since anyone had stirred her senses like this. She could see the firm thigh muscles straining against the expensive linen slacks as he reached her and took her arm.

'You must see the orchids. They're fantastic —the most beautiful orchids in the world!' He was propelling her along wide paths between vast expanses of greensward.

She could see Peking ducks and swans gliding gracefully on the ornamental lake. 'Oh, do stop for a moment, Simon.' His name had come quite naturally to her lips and she watched his expression.

'Later; we'll see the orchids first.' He quickened the pace.

Always in a hurry! thought Anna breathlessly.

Even in this idyllic place, he must keep to a schedule.

'There! Aren't they beautiful!' he announced triumphantly, as they went into the orchid garden.

Anna had to admit that the inordinate rush had been worth it. On every side she could feast her eyes on the delicate, exotic blooms. She stared in wonder at the amazing sight and breathed in the heady perfume.

Simon led her into the orchid house where there were souvenirs for sale. She was desperately aware of his hand under her elbow as she paused to examine a golden orchid necklace.

'Would you like to buy this for your wife, sir?' The salesgirl was already holding out the necklace for Anna to try on.

Oh, my God, I hope he doesn't think I'm trying to get him to buy me something! she thought, as she tried to take a step backwards. But he was right behind her and she couldn't move. Her movement had merely increased their proximity. She could feel his hot breath on the back of her hair.

'We take a fresh orchid and dip it in gold,' the girl was saying, oblivious to the turmoil she was creating. 'This one is very beautiful; only thirty-eight Singapore dollars . . .'

'I'll take it,' said Simon decisively, peeling off a handful of notes.

'Shall I put it in a box, sir?'

'No, let's see what it looks like.' He was reaching out to take the necklace with his long, tapering fingers.

Anna held her breath as she felt his fingers on the back of her neck, fastening the slender gold chain. And then he had spun her round to face him. His blue eyes were tender as she dared to raise her own

'I like it.' His voice was husky.

'You really shouldn't buy me presents. I hope you don't think I . . .'

'I like buying presents; especially for attractive young women.'

He makes it sound so casual, Anna thought. means such a lot to me, and to him it means nothing.

'Thank you. It's lovely,' she said quietly.

And so are you, Simon was thinking reluctantly I don't suppose your husband has the cash to buy you presents. I only hope he won't interpret m impulsive gesture. Oh well, he could always sell i

'Let's go and see the lake.' He moved away from her and she followed.

Heavy clouds had gathered in the evening sky obliterating the twilight rays of the sun. He turne to wait for her.

'We'll have to get a move on—it's going to rair Even as he spoke, the heavy rain spots came tum bling down in drenching streaks. It was as if som one had suddenly turned on the shower. He put a arm protectively around her waist, exhorting her run as quickly as she could.

'We'll make for that cabin by the lake—ov there!' he shouted, his arm tightening its hold.

She could feel the strength of him floodi through her as she ran. All she had to do was mo her legs and he took her with him. They were bo laughing as the warm tropical rain ran down th faces and drenched their clothes. It took only se onds to reach the cabin, but they were complete soaked.

'There's nothing we can do except sit it out.' I

guided her to a wooden bench inside the rustic cabin.

Anna sank down on it breathlessly. 'Phew, that was fun!' Her eyes were alight with exhilaration as she turned to face him, her cheeks damp and shining in the twilight.

'I thought so too,' he laughed as he pulled a large man-size handkerchief from his trouser pocket and started to mop his brow. 'It's wet through!' He wrung out the dripping cloth, and Anna laughed hysterically.

'If you could only see yourself . . .' she began, but he pulled her suddenly towards him, his hand pushing back the wet hair from her forehead.

'You look like a mermaid!' He was grinning as he stared into her dark brown eyes. 'Perhaps I should throw you into the water . . .'

He looked as if he were about to scoop her up. She screamed in mock despair and he leaned forward to silence her lips with a brief kiss.

It's all a game, she told herself, as he leaned back against the wooden wall. He's simply amusing himself . . . but I haven't felt so alive before . . .

'I think it's stopping,' he announced quickly.

Anna was wet through, but she wanted the rain to go on for ever. The huge drops on the surface of the lake were becoming smaller. A brilliant blue and green kingfisher dived down, took a shiny grey fish in its beak and swooped upwards again, as swiftly as it had arrived. Two black swans with bright red beaks swam leisurely past them towards the tall straight reeds at the edge of the lake. A couple of ducks walked solemnly by, ignoring the bouncing rain as they searched the puddles for worms. A terrapin was swimming near the surface,

its dear little face turned towards the dying rays of
the sun, which was peeping from behind a large
grey cloud.

'We could make a dash for the car. Here, take my
hand,' said Simon, thinking that if they stayed here
much longer he might do something he would
regret. He didn't want to spoil a good professional
relationship.

Anna's legs felt weak as they dashed back to
the car. The damp dress clung round her knees,
impeding her flight. As she climbed into the car she
realised that she was actually shivering.

'Don't put the air-conditioning on—I'm cold!'
she told him.

He laughed. 'In this heat?'

'But it's true,' she stammered. 'Why else would I
be shivering?'

He started up the car. 'As your personal phys-
ician, I prescribe a warm bath, followed by a
Singapore Sling. We'll go to Raffles Hotel.'

Her mouth opened wide, but not a sound was
uttered. Were they actually going to stay at the
famous hotel where royalty, film stars, poets and
writers had stayed? It was like a dream! She closed
her eyes, hoping she wouldn't wake up . . .

'Here we are,' she heard him say.

They were driving into a semi-circular driveway;
huge stone columns dwarfed the elegant open
doors; white-coated stewards were waiting to welcome them. Simon turned off the engine and tossed
the keys to one of the attendants. Anna's door was
being opened and there was nothing for it but to
step out, in her filthy, wet, offwhite dress and look
as if she was used to this sort of luxury.

'This way, Anna.'

She was grateful for the comforting arm under her elbow as she made her entrance. Simon seemed oblivious to the state of his clothes as he made for the long reception desk.

'Two single rooms for tonight.' His tone was brisk and yet casual as he dazzled the receptionist with his smile.

'We have two Palm Court superior rooms on the first floor or . . .'

'Do they overlook the gardens?' he broke in.

'But of course, sir.'

'I'll take them. My name is Sinclair. Let me use your phone.' He was holding out his hand impatiently. 'Put me through to the National University Hospital.'

The receptionist didn't argue. This client might be in a bedraggled state, but he was certainly someone who was used to ordering people around!

Anna watched his face anxiously as he enquired about Magdi.

'Well?' she asked quickly, as he put the phone down.

'Ralph's still operating on him. Sister said she would get him to call me when he's finished.' He looked worried.

'It's taking rather a long time, isn't it?' she put in gently.

'It's a difficult operation,' he snapped, then added in a more congenial voice, 'Let's go and clean up.'

Her shoes resounded on the tiled floor as they walked down a wide corridor to a flight of stairs. Then they were walking along a rich ruby red carpet beside the doors to the first-floor bedrooms. One side of the corridor was open, giving a view of the Tiffin Room. Above her was another balcony corridor and above that the high ceiling, domed to the moonlit sky.

'Meet me in the Long Bar in half an hour,' said Simon brusquely, as the steward opened the doors to their rooms.

Anna went inside, wondering if she should tip the immaculate white-coated man who had placed her shabby bag on the luxurious carpet. But he was already turning away, preparing to leave. I expect Simon's taken care of it, she thought thankfully, as she gazed round the spacious room.

She walked across the thick blue carpet to the balcony overlooking the gardens. Below her she could hear the murmur of voices and the clink of glasses. The rain had vanished and a warm steamy perfume of bougainvillea assailed her nostrils. She turned back into the room, trailing her fingers across the white surface of a wrought iron table on which someone had placed a huge bunch of roses. There were a couple of comfortable armchairs, their cushions picking up the identical blue shade of the carpet. Through an archway, she found her bed—and gasped at the ornate splendour of the drapes surrounding it.

She went through into the blue and white bathroom beyond, thinking, as she peeled off her sodden dress, that it was like going back in time to a bygone age when the leisured traveller accepted such luxury as the norm. She remembered reading somewhere that Somerset Maugham, Noël Coward and Rudyard Kipling had all stayed here. The hot water gushed out of the shining taps as she stepped into the enormous bath, sprinkling it liberally, with sweet-smelling bath salts. She lay back in the soft foam and closed her eyes . . . Bliss! . . . but she mustn't fall asleep . . .

The sound of rushing water came to her through the wall. We must have adjoining bathrooms, she thought, and her pulse quickened at the thought of Simon climbing into his bath only a few feet away from her. But as she remembered him, she decided she had better get a move on. Mustn't be late! I wonder where the Long Bar is . . .

She had no difficulty finding it. A deferential waiter in the corridor led her straight there. Simon rose to greet her. Two large, bulbous glasses of pink liquid, topped with white froth and decorated with a slice of pineapple, a cherry and the distinctive green Raffles cocktail stick appeared on their glass-topped cane table, as if by magic.

'Your Singapore slings, sir,' said the waiter, retiring back to the bar as quickly as he had arrived.

'Cheers!' Simon was smiling at her as he raised his glass.

She took a small sip and grinned back at him. 'Wow!' Her inhibitions seemed to vanish instantaneously. 'That tastes good.' She looked at the pink shade of her drink, thinking it was almost the identical shade of her skirt and blouse.

When the glass was half empty, she decided that her clothes didn't look too out of place, after all. Not the height of chic—she'd bought them in the little store in the main street of Penasing—but glancing round, she saw that no one else seemed to be done up to the nines either. There was a much more casual atmosphere in the Long Bar than she had expected. Behind the bar she could see a huge mural depicting the old colonial days; there was an elegant Victorian lady with a parasol and an over-

dressed gentleman, sporting a drooping moustache. Strange to think that people like that must
have stayed here . . .

'How are you feeling now?' Simon's bedside-
manner voice broke in on her thoughts.

'Marvellous!' She turned to him with shining
eyes.

'I don't think our shower in the Botanic Gardens
will have harmed us,' he pronounced, as if he were
presenting her with a medical decision. He drained
his glass. 'Would you like another one?'

'Good heavens, no!' she laughed. Her head felt
quite light.

'Drink up, then. We'll go in to dinner.'

Anna followed her boss reluctantly. It would
have been nice to stay a while longer soaking up the
fascinating atmosphere. She glanced up at the high
ceiling as they were leaving the room, unwilling to
miss even the smallest detail. Huge fans were whirring above them, blowing the leaves of the plants in
the hanging baskets and moving the colourful
Chinese lanterns from side to side.

'This way, Anna,' said Simon, taking hold of her
arm firmly.

She felt like a child on a Sunday School outing,
being dragged along so quickly that she couldn't
absorb all the exciting, unfamiliar experiences.
They walked a few paces along the corridor to the
Elizabethan Grill Room. A waiter ushered them to
a corner table and lit the candles. There was a rustle
of starched white tablecloth as she sat down next to
the rich oak-panelled wall.

'What are you going to have?' Simon asked.

Her eyes scanned the long menu. 'What do you
suggest?' she replied cagily.

'We could have the traditional Raffles menu.'

'Sounds great.' She closed the book and handed it back to the waiter.

'We'll have a bottle of Muscadet with the fish and a bottle of Château les Moines with the beef,' Simon instructed him.

'Very good, sir.' The waiter scuttled off and returned with the traditional bill of fare menu.

'I hope I can eat all this,' said Anna, as she looked down the page with a giggle. The Singapore Sling had gone to her head and she felt deliciously relaxed.

The bill of fare was printed in old-style script and boldly announced that they were to have:

Clear Soup Windsor
Dover Sole St. George
Ye Sire-Loin of Olde England
Hertfordshire Prime Yorkshire Pudding
Cornwall Cauliflower, Butter Sauce
Baked Lincolnshire Potatoes
Devonshire Strawberries with Cream

The soup arrived before Anna had finished reading. She suddenly realised she was starving and tucked into it with relish. As she put down her spoon she saw that Simon had been watching her and blushed with embarrassment.

'No need to ask if you enjoyed that,' he said with a knowing smile, thinking how nice it was to take out a girl who liked her food. So many of the girls he escorted were on permanent diets and talked endlessly about boring calories and the disastrous effect they had on their figures. This girl looked as if she could eat as much as she liked and never put on an ounce. He topped up her wine glass. Anna was about to remonstrate, but decided she might as well enjoy herself. They were off duty, after all.

'We'll have a pause,' Simon said to the waiter, between the main course and the dessert. He took out a cigar and the waiter leaned forward to light it.

'I don't approve of smoking,' he said, in answer to the surprised query in Anna's eyes. 'But I indulge myself with a cigar on special occasions.'

'And is this a special occasion?' she asked, emboldened by the wine.

'I'd like to think so,' he replied quickly, hoping she wouldn't misinterpret his remark. Perhaps he was overdoing things, but he did so want to give the girl a good time. He had felt so sorry for the way she had grasped desperately at his offer of a lucrative job. It couldn't be easy being a working wife when you were hard up, he thought, as he scrutinised her face in the candlelight.

'Tell me about your husband; is he an understanding man?' he asked cautiously, not wanting to appear as if he were too interested.

She gave a puzzled frown. 'He died three years ago—in a car crash.'

'I'm sorry . . . I had no idea,' Simon stammered. How stupid of him not to have checked!

'Of course you didn't know. I never talk about it if I can help it. It happened, that's all, and now I'm alone again—or rather, I wish I were!'

He was surprised at the bitterness in her voice, but he didn't want to ask questions. Her eyes were dry, but he had the feeling that she was crying inside.

'My mother-in-law was paralysed in the accident and I have to take care of her,' she continued, in a deadpan tone. 'I pay for a nursing attendant to live in and domestic help twice a week. But there's still an awful lot to do when I go home, and the emotional strain is exhausting sometimes.'

She broke off and stared up at him, wondering why she was telling him all this. He wouldn't want to be burdened with her problems. All he had asked was if her husband was understanding, and she hadn't answered his question. But was Ibrahim understanding? she asked herself, and pulled a wry grin. In the early days, yes, he was, but later . . . she had to admit, he had changed beyond recognition. He had been a tyrant.

Simon mistook her sad look. She must miss her husband terribly, he thought, and on impulse, he reached across the table and covered her tiny hand with his own.

'Don't worry, Anna. You're young—you'll find someone else,' he began softly, but she pulled away her hand as if she had been stung.

'No! I'll never love again—I can't; it wouldn't be fair,' she blurted, and immediately wished she hadn't. How could she explain her conviction that it would be wrong to condemn a man to a childless marriage?

He stared at her, puzzled by her words. 'Fair to whom?' he asked softly.

'I don't want to talk about it. Anyway, the question will never arise, because I'm tied to Safiah, my mother-in-law. I'm all she has left of her favourite son and she depends on me not to let her down.'

The waiter was hovering discreetly in the background. As he saw Simon Sinclair stub out his cigar he came forward.

'Shall I bring your dessert, sir?' he asked, with a slight, deferential bow.

Simon looked across the table and Anna shook her head. Suddenly the idea of strawberries and cream had palled.

'We'll just have coffee,' he said, vowing not to ask any more questions that evening.

'Dr Sinclair?' A second waiter was crossing the room.

Simon was on his feet, knowing that it had to be the phone call from Ralph James. As the waiter confirmed his surmise he strode to the telephone beyond the archway.

Anna waited at the table, desperate for news of her little patient. She watched the surgeon's face as he returned from the phone. The firm, handsome features were giving nothing away.

'How is Magdi?' she asked quickly, as he resumed his seat.

'He's in intensive care,' he replied shortly. 'Ralph has removed a massive thoracic sarcoma. He wants to keep him in for a few weeks.'

'A few weeks?' she echoed. 'But why?'

'He'll have to undergo radiotherapy treatment. We must be sure we've eradicated all the malignancy.'

'His poor granny!' whispered Anna, almost under her breath. 'She'll be so worried when she knows.'

'I think the rest will do her good,' was his realistic response. 'She's had a tough time coping with an infant by herself. Magdi will be in the best place for the next few weeks. But we'll go over to Desaman when we get back to Malaysia, to explain the situation.'

Why did her heart flutter at the thought of another trip with this disturbing man? She had just told him of her complete indifference to the opposite sex, and yet here she was, already trembling with excitement at the prospect of being near him again. She would have to keep a tighter rein on her emotions, she told herself vehemently as she watched him signing the bill.

She had declined his offer of a brandy, realising that she had already drunk far more than she was used to. It was clouding her judgment. Any minute now she might give in to her impulses and reveal the depth of her feelings, and that would never do. She wanted to remain friendly with her boss—nothing more, she told herself firmly. He was the sort of man she admired professionally and, if things had been different, she would have allowed herself to fall for him—though heaven knows what he'd see in me! she thought. I couldn't possibly interest a man like that—even if I were free.

She swayed as she stood up and Simon grabbed her arm. 'Steady on,' he murmured, smiling down into her brown eyes. She blinked up at him.

'I do believe I'm a bit tipsy. Must have been the wine . . . I'm not used to drinking . . . and the Singapore Sling—what on earth do they put in them?'

He grinned as she clutched on to his arm. 'It's a mixture of gin, Benedictine, Cointreau, lime juice . . .'

'That's enough,' she interrupted. 'I think you'd better take me to bed—I mean, back to my room.'

Simon paused by her door, his arm still about her waist. 'Are you sure you'll be all right?' he asked gently.

'I feel wonderful!' was her reassuring reply, as she fumbled in her bag for her key.

He took it from her and opened the door. He was sorely tempted to invite himself in, but it would only create problems, and Anna was too good a nurse to lose. Better keep her at arm's length, he thought wistfully, as he dropped a kiss on her forehead, as nonchalantly as possible under the circumstances.

She smiled and automatically raised her face upwards, as if in a dream. I'll regret this tomorrow, thought Simon, but even so, he lowered his head and kissed her full on the lips.

She seemed to awake from a deep sleep. He saw her wide brown eyes staring into his as he raised his head.

'Good night, Anna, he said brusquely. 'I'll see you at eight o'clock sharp, in the Tiffin Room.' And with that, he beat a hasty retreat, cursing himself for his weakness.

Anna went into her room, her heart pounding. Simon's kiss had removed all feeling of inebriation. She felt stone cold sober—and much too happy! She went out on to the balcony and sat on a cushioned wrought-iron seat, gazing at the floodlit gardens. On the adjoining balcony she heard someone pulling heavily on a cigar. Simon's strong outline was framed in the moonlight as he gripped the railing.

Another special occasion! she thought wickedly, as she watched the glow from his cigar, unaware that she was the source of his inner turmoil. Simon dragged on his cigar and stared out across the moonlit garden as he tried desperately to resolve the conflict within himself. His hands gripped the iron railing of the ornate balcony and beads of sweat broke out on his forehead.

I mustn't give in now! he told himself vehemently, remembering all the years he had fanned the flames over his personal vendetta. Emotional involvement is out until I've settled my score, he resolved grimly. I'm so near—so near and yet so far!

He knew that the man he was searching for was in Malaysia and until recently had been employed at Kedang hospital. His recent enquiries had ascertained that the charlatan had been dismissed for his drinking habits. After his dismissal, the hospital had discovered charges amounting to criminal negligence, but Doktor Smith, as he called himself, had disappeared. Simon wanted to see him brought to justice for personal reasons. The bogus doctor had robbed him of his first love; he had promised himself he wouldn't fall in love again until he had avenged this.

He sank down on to one of the wicker chairs and puffed a blue ring of smoke into the air as he thought of the number of occasions over the years when he had thought about giving in. There had been mild flirtations, a few passionate encounters, but no one had stirred his interest like Anna was doing.

Suddenly he tossed his cigar to the stone floor and ground it with his shoe. Damn the girl! he told himself decisively. She's not going to upset my plans.

Thank God she isn't free, he thought wryly as he turned to go inside.

CHAPTER FOUR

SIMON WAS strangely quiet at breakfast time. Anna decided he was regretting his impulsive kiss of the night before, and she was absolutely right! So she had only her own thoughts to occupy her as she stared round at the white columns with their ornate gold décor, the crystal chandeliers, the whirring fans and the sun shining through the glass in the high domed ceiling. She toyed with half a grapefruit and a piece of toast until Simon announced that it was time to go.

She hovered at the back of the spacious lobby as he settled the bill. It was cool beside the potted plants, but she could see the hot sun blazing down on the gardens outside. A steward had brought the blue car to the door and was waiting courteously to finish his duties.

Simon pressed some dollars into his hand as he slid into the driver's seat.

'Thank you, sir.' The young steward smiled and held the door for Anna.

They glided out through the palm-fringed entrance and surged forward amid the morning traffic along Beach Road. Anna breathed a sigh of relief as the density of vehicles thinned along the dual carriageway. They were turning into Lower Kent Ridge Road when Simon announced,

'We'll call at the hospital and take a look at Magdi.'

'Good. I shall feel happier when I've seen him for

myself,' said Anna, fixing her white cap on her head and smoothing down the skirt of her uniform dress. With typical efficiency, a Raffles maid had washed and ironed it overnight. She inspected the white cotton carefully and could find no trace of the storm stains. It's as if it never happened, she told herself. Perhaps it was a dream . . .

'Jump out; I'll park the car,' said a brusque voice. Simon, impatiently wondering why the girl was daydreaming again, reached across and pushed open her door to speed things up.

They were directed along a maze of spotless white corridors to Intensive Care, while a frantic receptionist paged Ralph James to tell him that his surgeon colleague had arrived. Anna stared down at the tiny scrap, swathed in dressings. Only his little brown face was peeping out of the mass of sterile cloth, and that was attached to various tubes. She glanced at the monitoring screen.

'His heartbeat is steady,' she said, in a relieved voice.

'Yes, he seems to be holding his own,' Simon murmured as he glanced at Magdi's charts.

Ralph James came through the swing doors, breathless from his rush from theatre. They had caught him between operations and he would have to scrub up again. But there were several points he wanted to discuss with his colleague.

The two men conferred gravely. It seemed that there was a good chance that the tumour had been removed in time to save Magdi's life.

'The histology reveals malignancy,' Ralph explained, 'But we have no reason to suppose, at this stage, that there's evidence of dissemination of the malignant cells. However, if secondaries do show up, then I'm afraid the outlook is bleak.'

Anna stifled the urge to wipe back a tear that had strayed on to her cheek. Nurses weren't supposed to cry over their patients, but little Magdi was sort of special, she told herself, by way of excuse. She blew him a kiss, and felt embarrassed as both surgeons unexpectedly turned.

Ralph James smiled and stroked his beard. 'Was that meant for me, nurse?' he asked glibly.

'Oh, I'm sorry, sir . . .'

'Please don't apologise, my dear. It was the nicest thing that's happened to me all week.' He paused, his hand on the door. 'I'll be in touch, Simon.' And as he went out of the door, the elder surgeon couldn't help thinking what a lucky man his colleague was.

Simon deliberately made no allusion to the incident as he hurried ahead to the car. He was trying to distance himself from Nurse Gabell and wishing he'd checked her background before he'd appointed her. If he'd known she was a widow —and a young, attractive one at that—he would have thought twice about the appointment. But the fact that she takes her duties to the family seriously, and this other unknown factor that's put her against emotional commitment, are definitely in her favour, he was thinking, as he unlocked the stuffy car. Nevertheless, a few days of hospital routine will be a good thing to get life back into perspective . . .

Anna was thinking exactly the same thing about her return to hospital. She couldn't wait to leave the arrogant doctor on their arrival at Penasing. He had remained silent throughout the journey and she had been reluctant to put herself at the mercy of his sarcastic wit. She had stared out of the window at the miles and miles of lush jungle, longing to be back on the ward.

Her little patients greeted her with cries of delight, and Staff Nurse Wong was over the moon at the prospect of some off-duty.

'Sister Kasim asked me to do a double shift today,' she moaned, 'but now that you're back, I can have the afternoon off.'

'It's so nice to feel welcome,' smiled Anna. 'Give me a report and then run along and enjoy yourself.'

Five minutes later she was alone with her patients and their relatives. It's good to be back, she thought, as she passed between the beds and cots, making herself conversant with the state of each child. Little Hayati reached up and gave her an impromptu hug.

'I've missed you,' she whispered in Malay to her favourite nurse. It had seemed a long time since yesterday.

Anna was thinking exactly the same thing. It seemed like a lifetime since she had set off for Singapore. It was surprising how things could change in twenty-four hours.

Her welcome at home was less ecstatic. The old matriarch complained that she had been neglected while Anna was away.

'Well, if you'd prefer me to abandon this new job . . .' she began knowingly, only to be interrupted with protestations.

'No, no, Anna. You have your career to follow!'

And you'd miss the extra money, Anna thought, as she watched the old lady's scheming face. She tucked her into bed, placed a glass of water near at hand and with a dutiful, 'Good night, Mother,' she went downstairs.

Razali had returned and was sitting out on the back porch, a glass of fruit juice in his hand.

'Razali! I didn't know you were home . . .'

'Ssh! Don't waken the old dear—I can't face her tonight. Besides, I want to tell you the good news first. I had a phone call at the office today. I've got the job in Singapore!' His face was shining with excitement.

'That's wonderful! When do you start?' Anna asked him.

'Next month. Won't Mother be pleased!'

'Yes, she will,' she said, in a guarded voice. Her mind was already leaping ahead to the problems his absence would create—but she would cross that bridge when she came to it. In the meantime she wanted Razali to enjoy his well-earned triumph. He deserved it. She reached up and kissed his cheek.

'Well done!' she pronounced, smiling at his happiness.

It was several days until her next meeting with Simon Sinclair. She heard that he had flown off again to one of the islands, and she told herself she hoped he would stay there for a long time. When he wandered into the ward one hot afternoon she stared at him in surprise.

'I thought you were away,' she began lamely, then wished she had greeted his appearance with cold indifference. He must surely hear the sound of her thumping heart.

'Is your bag packed?' he asked, his blue eyes daring her to give him a negative reply.

'Of course,' she answered quickly. Since that first

light to Singapore she had made a point of keeping
bag at the ready.

'Well, that's an improvement. I'm glad you're
aking this job seriously. 'We're off to Desaman.
Sister Kasim is sending a replacement for you.'

As he spoke, one of the nurses from Casualty
arrived.

'I'll give her a report . . .' Anna began.

'Nurse Wong can do that. Come *now*! I might
have to do a Caesar. They've radioed through to
say there's a patient who's been in labour several
hours already . . . And she's a breech presentation,' Simon added breathlessly, as they left the
ward together.

'Why don't you have her flown over here?' asked
Anna, her mind focusing on the new medical
problem.

'Because it's not as straightforward as that,' he
snapped mysteriously.

'I'll get my bag.' They were level with her changing room and Anna left the impatient doctor
fuming outside while she delved in the depths of her
locker.

She put on a deliberately bright smile as she
emerged. No point in getting on the wrong side of
him, she thought as she looked up into the bright
blue eyes.

An ambulance was waiting for them outside
Casualty, and they tore through the centre of
Penasing, sirens blaring, and out to the tiny airstrip. Anna swallowed hard as she saw the ancient
four-seater aircraft. Well, there's a first time for
everything, she thought nervously, as she followed the tall figure of the surgeon out across the
tarmac.

She closed her eyes as she heard the uneven revving of the engines.

'You look as if you're praying,' said a sardonic voice beside her.

She turned to look at him, her teeth chattering. 'I *am* praying,' she muttered. 'I'm praying to God, Allah, the saints from my old convent school and anybody else who might be up there!'

Simon laughed. 'You'll have them totally confused if you're not careful.' He leaned over and patted her hand, comfortingly, as if she were a child.

She grabbed hold of it and clung on for dear life as the little plane lurched forward. Within seconds they were airborne, and through her half-closed eyes Anna could see the azure blue of the sea shining beneath them. It was so beautiful that she forgot to be afraid and opened her eyes wide in amazement. The next instant she dropped the surgeon's hand, as if it were scorching hot. How could she have been so uninhibited!

She turned to glance at his face and was relieved to see that he was smiling.

'There, that wasn't so bad, was it?' His voice was gentle—almost tender, she noticed, and warning bells sounded in her ears. Be careful, she told herself firmly. Don't let him get through to you. Stay calm and professional . . .

As they skimmed low over the water she could see the brightly coloured sails of a fishing prahu shining in the late afternoon sun. One of the crew, tiny as a doll, waved upwards at the huge grey mechanical bird, and she waved back, although she doubted if he would see her.

'There's Desaman!' Simon called to her, above

the cacophony of the engines.

Anna saw the outline of a wild, rugged island reaching up into the clouds. A heavy rainstorm was clearing from the mountainsides and as the sun broke through, a spectacular rainbow reached down from the sky and touched the shoreline.

'I've never been above a rainbow before,' she cried excitedly, looking down at the vivid arc merging with the waves.

'Neither have I,' he said, taking a vicarious pleasure from her enthusiasm.

'Do you think we'll find a crock of gold on the shore there?' she asked, grinning mischievously up into the blue eyes.

'If we look hard enough, I expect we will,' he replied in a husky voice. He too had planned to remain detached from this appealing young woman, but there was something about her that weakened his resolve. He cleared his throat. 'That's the village where our patient lives,' he said in a firm, professional tone.

Anna looked along the shore, but before she could pick out the group of wooden houses the plane started to dive down towards the hillside. It appeared as if they would crash into the dense green jungle. She closed her eyes, hoping the young pilot, at the controls just in front of her, knew what he was doing. Seconds later she felt a violent change of direction and opened her eyes in panic. The plane had turned, at the last moment, and was heading for the narrow airstrip.

'Does he always do that?' she asked Simon breathlessly.

'He laughed at her petrified face. 'I'm afraid so—you'll get used to it. It's the only way he can approach the runway. Don't worry; he's very experienced for his age. And the other chap is his instructor . . .'

'You mean he's still under instruction?' She had lowered her voice, but there was no need. The engines drowned their conversation.

'Got to have a first time for everything,' he replied with a grin. 'It was the first time he'd taken the controls for this flight . . .'

'And you knew! And you didn't tell me!' Her voice rose to a shriek.

The co-pilot instructor turned with a frown to see if there was a problem, but Simon was quick to reassure him.

'My nurse would like to compliment your trainee on his excellence . . .' he began, but the sound was lost in the downward thrust of the engines. The plane touched down with a bump, rose in the air for a few yards, then landed on the narrow strip and taxied to a halt.

As she walked away from the aircraft, Anna discovered she was trembling. Simon noticed it too, and put an arm round her shoulder.

The feel of his hand touching her upper arm sent shivers down her spine. She was glad when they walked into the tiny control hut and he had to remove it.

'We need a boat to take us to the village,' he began, but the helpful Malay official was already out of the hut, beckoning them to follow him.

Anna heard the words, 'My brother will take you in his boat,' and felt thankful that someone always seemed to have a useful brother in this part of the world.

As they skimmed over the water in the fishing

boat, Simon explained that it was the quickest way of getting to the village.

'There is a path along the seashore, but it's often impassable after the monsoon rains and it's always very slow,' he told her as she gazed across the bay towards the cluster of wooden huts, grouped together by the sea. They were all built on low stilts to prevent flooding and the roofs were thatched with brown reeds.

As they reached the beach, a small thin, wiry man came running across the pebbles, oblivious to the discomfort of his brown feet.

'*Doktor, doktor!*' he was shouting, his voice a mixture of anguish and relief at seeing the arrival of medical help for his poor suffering wife.

'It's okay, Mohammed; I'm here—and this is my nurse, Anna,' said Simon, giving the distraught father-to-be a firm handshake. 'How is Kandiah?'

Anna gathered that his wife had been in labour for hours. It didn't look so good.

They hurried to Mohammed's house, which was at the edge of the tiny village. An old woman greeted them as they went into the dim interior, and in her eyes Anna could read the fear that she felt over this difficult birth. She had delivered many babies in her long life, but she was fearing the worst over this one. She stepped back to allow the clever doctor to take a look at her daughter, but doubting that there was anything he could do.

'Bring me some hot water,' Simon said quickly. He smiled down at the young woman and Anna reached forward to wipe the patient's perspiring face. She took the bowl of hot water from the old lady and they both scrubbed up as best they could.

As she was preparing the instruments, Simon made his examination.

'I'll have to do a Caesarian section under epidural,' he whispered to Anna. He explained what he was going to do to the patient as briefly as possible, in Malay. The poor young woman had reached the stage at which she no longer cared what happened so long as the pain stopped.

Simon nodded to Anna. 'Turn her on her side,' he muttered.

She held the patient towards her as he inserted the local anaesthetic into the epidural space. Then she rolled her on to her back and spread a sterile towel over the abdomen. There was no time for the routine preparations in an emergency like this, she thought desperately. She had heard the foetal heartbeat with her Pinard's stethoscope. It was above the umbilicus, as she would have expected in a breech presentation. The baby was still alive. It was up to Simon to see that it remained so . . .

He was swabbing the skin preparatory to the first incision. The patient had closed her eyes, thankful that the pain had stopped and oblivious to all that was going on. Her husband and her mother had, on the suggestion of the doctor, retired outside and were sitting on the wooden steps, praying quietly, their faces turned towards Mecca.

Anna stemmed the initial flow of blood, holding back the skin with her forceps.

'I'll make an incision in the lower segment of the uterus,' Simon told her.

She watched his skilful fingers, hardly daring to breathe as he grasped the tiny body and delivered it through the abdominal wall into her waiting hands. As she held the newborn infant, Simon quickly put his hand back into the uterus to separate the placenta from the uterine wall.

The next few minutes were crucial as they worked together to save the mother and baby. As Simon closed the abdominal wound, Anna held the baby for his mother to see. She was too weak to hold him, but her eyes shone with happiness.

The father and grandmother had drifted back inside, standing awkwardly in the doorway.

'It's a boy, and he's healthy,' the doctor told them, and watched their amazed reaction with satisfaction.

The old lady insisted it was a miracle. Their prayers had been answered—but the good doctor had been a great help too, she hastened to add in her most polite Malay.

The good doctor ran a hand over his damp dark hair. 'Is there anything to drink in this place?' he asked, suddenly remembering how thirsty he was.

The old lady ran outside and they could hear her cracking a coconut. When they had made sure that mother and baby could be left for a while, they went out into the bright sunshine and accepted the bowls of coconut milk.

'What an idyllic setting!' Anna gazed around her at the lush palm trees which framed the white sandy beach. 'It looks like the perfect place to get away from it all.'

She sank down on to a large boulder, being careful not to spill her thirst-quenching coconut milk. Simon squatted down on the sand nearby, watching her through narrowed eyes.

'It's the perfect place to catch every disease under the sun,' he said, 'but somehow they manage to cock a snook at Mother Nature. It's only when they come up against something like the case we've just dealt with that they cry for help.'

He sighed and leaned back on the warm sand, stretching out his long, athletic legs in front of him. 'If only they'd taken my advice when I gave it last week, this need never have happened,' he continued, running a hand absently through the soft sand.

Anna had turned to watch him, unconsciously moved at the sight of his muscular frame. 'Yes, why wasn't she brought over to the hospital?' she asked quickly.

'Her mother had persuaded her it was dangerous,' he replied, trying to disguise his annoyance. 'Apparently, several years ago, someone from the village had been taken over to the mainland and had died in childbirth. I don't know any of the details except the fact that the incident has poisoned the minds of the islanders against us. I might tell you, I was jolly scared at the beginning of that Caesar . . .'

He broke off, ashamed at having made such an admission in front of his nurse. She has a way of worming things out of me, he thought, but when he looked at her he saw she was smiling at him tenderly.

'It didn't show,' she said softly, wanting to add that she thought he had been wonderful throughout the whole operation. There had been none of the bravado and theatrical gestures she had come to associate with routine hospital surgery. It had been a matter of life or death, and he had risen to the occasion. She was proud to have assisted him.

'We'd better get back.' Simon was standing up, shaking the soft sand from his cotton slacks. 'We've got to persuade them that Kandiah and the baby need a couple of weeks in hospital. I'll need your help in that, so think out your best Malay phrases. You women know more about the art of persuasion than we men,' he added with a wry grin.

Anna didn't know whether to take that as a compliment, as they crossed the threshold into the dark little hut. As her eyes adjusted from the bright sunlight, she saw that the old lady was trying to prop up her daughter, preparatory to commencing breast feeding.

'Not like that!' Anna moved quickly, aware of the discomfort that her patient was suffering from the abdominal wound. 'I'll help her,' she told the bewildered grandmother. 'She mustn't sit up yet. It's too soon.'

'But the baby must be fed,' answered the old lady stubbornly.

'Yes, I'll show you how.' Anna was patience itself as she turned Kandiah on to her side and held the tiny infant to her breast.

The wrinkled grandmother smiled as she saw the baby beginning to suck. Maybe the young nurse knows what she's talking about, she admitted to herself grudgingly. But she wasn't going to let them take her youngest daughter away from her. All the others had deserted her—gone to the mainland to make some money—but she was going to keep Kandiah near her so she would be cared for in her old age.

The sun was setting when they left the little wooden house. They were tired, but satisfied that mother and baby would survive the night. Mohammed had promised to call them if there was any problem. He showed them the path to a nearby hut.

In the failing light, Anna was relieved to see that it was bigger inside than it appeared from the outside. What was more important, there were two distinct rooms!

'I will bring you food,' said Mohammed, indicating that they were to sit at the table in front of their hut.

She realised all of a sudden that she was starving hungry. It had been a long time since lunch in the hospital canteen.

As they sat on the uneven wooden bench, they watched the sun dip down into the sea and disappear in a warm burning glow of fire. Darkness descended almost at once. The multi-coloured birds ceased their singing, the monkeys in the nearby forest stopped chattering among the trees, but the insects and lizards began their nocturnal noises as Simon lit the oil lamp on the table. The delicious smell of freshly caught fish, smoking over charcoal, drifted across and they knew Mohammed was cooking supper.

'You're sure that Sister Kasim won't forget to phone my mother-in-law?' she asked, not wanting to break the spell of the tropical evening by discussing mundane matters, but hoping to dispel the constant worry at the back of her mind.

'I've told you, Sister Kasim is extremely efficient,' Simon repeated patiently. 'As soon as I knew we were flying out here I asked her to put a call through. Tell me, what sort of medical care is your mother-in-law receiving?'

She looked surprised at his question. 'There's nothing more that can be done. She was told this at Kedang hospital, soon after the crash.'

'So in effect she hasn't been seen by a doctor

for . . . how long?' he prompted, his eyes shining with impatience.

'Three years,' Anna told him, wondering what the learned doctor was getting at.

'Doesn't that seem somewhat negligent?' he asked evenly.

'How dare you insinuate that I'm neglecting Safiah!' she protested. 'I work constantly to see that she wants for nothing . . .'

'Hold on!' He interrupted her tirade by reaching across to take her trembling hand in his. 'I'm sure you're doing everything you possibly can; my criticism was with the medic who pronounced her incurable and abandoned her to a wheelchair. Do you have any idea who was in charge of the case?'

'I'm afraid not. You see, I was a patient myself in the same hospital at the time,' she faltered, 'so none of the details were divulged to me until . . . later.'

'I'm sorry. What was the trouble?' As a medical man, Simon had to probe further. There was something that worried him about this case. And at the back of his mind he was beginning to link it to another situation of paramount importance to him.

'I had a miscarriage.' Anna's bland tone gave nothing away, but he sensed the misery of her revelation.

'I'm sorry,' he repeated, for the second time in a few seconds. 'That must have been awful for you at a time like that . . . Did you miscarry before or after the crash?'

'I don't want to talk about it,' she snapped. 'I'm not a patient giving a case history, you know.' She stopped quickly, as Mohammed appeared, carrying their supper.

'*Terima kasih*,' Simon said, smiling up at the gentle Malay. 'How is Kandiah?'

'She is sleeping, *doktor*,' replied Mohammed, setting down the food on the table.

There was grilled fish, rice, bananas, and coconut milk. The food was served on huge banana leaves. As soon as Mohammed returned to his hut they began their feast and the discussion appeared to have been forgotten. Simon scooped up the rice with his fingers, so Anna followed suit.

'That was delicious,' she pronounced, leaning back against the wall of their hut at the end of the meal. 'But my fingers feel very sticky. Where's the nearest water?'

'There's a fresh-water stream over there. You wash in the upper reaches and anything else in the lower section. We can bathe in the morning. I think we should turn in—the mosquitoes are starting to nibble.'

They washed their hands in the cool stream by the light of the moon. Anna felt terribly conscious of the large manly frame beside her. He was altogether too disturbing, she thought. Perhaps it would be a good idea to get up early and bathe by herself . . .

CHAPTER FIVE

IN SPITE of her intention to rise early, the morning sun was high above the little village when Anna awoke. The hut was quiet, no sound issuing from the other side of the partition. She remembered lying awake in the night listening to the sound of Simon's breathing. It had been impossible to sleep; the acrid fumes from the insecticide coil that he had lit by the doorway had stung the mucous membrane in her nostrils. She had held the small cotton sheet tightly round her, feeling far too hot, but not wanting to expose herself to a stray cockroach or the eyes of the doctor, if he should decide to go for a walk in the night.

She had told herself that the latter was extremely unlikely! They had both been so exhausted when they turned in that they had fallen into deep sleep on either side of the partition almost immediately. She smiled as she remembered how they were both making a supreme effort to keep their relationship on a professional basis. She wondered if Simon had any idea how she had to struggle not to find him attractive. Probably not, she thought, as she extracted herself from the cotton sheet. After her first initial sleep of exhaustion, she had spent the night awake with her thoughts, the eerie nocturnal sounds of the jungle and the waves on the shore. It was only towards daybreak that she had drifted off again.

And now he'll probably chide me for sleeping

late! she thought anxiously, as she stepped out into the bright sunlight. She made her way carefully along the rough path towards the stream.

'Come on in! The water's wonderful!'

Anna stared across at the lean, muscular body swimming in the wide section of the stream. Simon had covered himself with soap and the lather floated after him as he cut through the water with long sweeping strokes. From the ripples in the water she looked up to the clear blue sky. In spite of what Simon said about the incidence of disease, she still thought it was an idyllic spot!

He was swimming away from her, deliberately averting his eyes so that she could slip into the natural pool unnoticed. She glanced at the transparent water, wondering if it would conceal her nakedness. It hadn't occurred to her that she might need a bathing suit! And from where she was standing, she could see that Simon had dispensed with such an unnecessary garment. The object of the exercise, she told herself firmly, is to get clean. And after twenty-four hours in the tropics without a shower, she certainly needed it!

She dropped her robe on the bank and slid under the water. The cool soothing feeling of the total immersion was like a primaeval baptism. She wondered why she had even contemplated wearing clothes! Across the other side of the pool, Simon was treading water as he smiled in approval at her discarded inhibitions.

'Would you like to borrow my soap?' he called with a grin.

'Yes, please,' she called back as she held out her hand to catch it. Her own highly civilised toilet bag was sitting on the grassy bank and there was no wa he could reach it without climbing out.

The white bar of soap came hurtling through the air and she missed it by inches.

'It's OK . . . I'll get it.' Simon dived down and came up by her side, holding the captured bar triumphantly in his hand.

Their hands touched as she took it from him. She felt suddenly terribly vulnerable—and much too excited! His chest was covered in fine droplets of water that shone like diamonds in the brilliant sunshine. The hairs on his arms were standing up thick and wet, outlining the strong muscles. But the most unnerving of all was the tenderness in his expressive blue eyes.

'Did you sleep well?' he asked huskily. He too was aware of the dangerous situation. Only a few inches of water was separating them, and Anna was a very desirable woman. It had been a terrible strain spending the night so close, with only a thin partition between them.

'Yes, I slept,' she answered vaguely.

'You're still half asleep,' he said gently, as he reached over to push the wet hair away from her eyes.

She felt his cool fingers brush her face and drew in an audible breath. So she's not the ice maiden she pretends to be, he thought. Beneath that frigid exterior, she's made of real flesh and blood. He turned away, cursing himself for feeling proud of his discovery. It would only cause complications if he got involved with her now. He moved away decisively, and swam to the other side of the pool.

'Hurry up; we've got to go and see our patient,' he called brusquely.

Anna averted her eyes as the tall brown figure

emerged from the water and wrapped himself in a towel.

Business as usual! she thought, hearing the cool edge to his voice. 'Catch!' she called, tossing the soap towards the bank.

He deliberately ignored her attempt to prolong the childish playtime. 'Bring it with you,' he called over his shoulder as he strode off back to the hut.

She was hurt by his change of mood and wondered what it was that had changed it.

That girl would require an emotional commitment, Simon thought as he lengthened his barefoot stride, and that's something I can't give . . . yet! He went into the hut and rubbed the towel briskly over himself. Anyway, she's much too complicated, he told himself decisively. By the time he'd resolved his own personal vendetta, he wouldn't want to start sorting out her problems!

Anna was glad the hut was empty when she got back from her bathe. She put Simon's soap down on the table to dry off. The spicy aroma enveloped her. It was a distinctive fragrance she would find difficult to forget, she thought ruefully; sort of heady and virile. It had been a mistake to borrow it . . . far safer to have used her own.

He was dressing Kandiah's abdominal wound when she caught up with him.

'Get rid of this dirty dressing, nurse,' he muttered as soon as she appeared on the scene.

'Yes, sir,' she replied automatically, and the professional rôles were resumed.

It took all their powers of persuasion before the old lady would allow her daughter to be taken to the mainland. Only when Anna pointed out that

e could come too did they reach an agreement.
he wrinkled old face broke into a smile and she
odded. And I'll go and see my other children
hile I'm over there, she thought to herself hap-
ly. She hadn't been to Penasing since before she
as married . . .

Simon arranged for the hire of a fishing boat to
rry them all over the water. It would take longer
an by air, but it would be more comfortable for
e patient. Anna felt relieved when he told her;
e had been steeling herself for the return flight all
r nothing!

'Is there time for me to meet Magdi's grand-
other before we leave?' she asked hopefully. She
new that Simon had already been over to the
land to report on their little patient's operation in
ingapore, but she would dearly like to meet the
d lady and help to give her some reassurance
out the case.

'I was about to suggest it. But we must hurry—
want to get Kandiah to hospital as quickly as
ossible. Follow me.'

Anna quickened her step along the dusty path
rough the village. A startled hen squawked out of
e way as they reached the tiny hut. Magdi's
randmother was sitting on the wooden steps
roking a large tabby cat.

'*Selamat pagi*—good morning,' Simon began.

The old lady shook the cat from her lap and
eached out both hands to grasp the doctor's. 'How
Magdi?' she asked, in Malay. 'When is he coming
ome?'

Simon had to explain that he hadn't been to
ingapore since he was last with her, but he was in
aily touch with the hospital and Magdi was making

good progress. If she wanted, he could arrange for her to visit her grandson. He would arrange the expenses and lay on transport—in fact, he would take her over to the mainland now if she liked . . .

The grandmother waved her hand and shook her head. Singapore was the end of the earth to her. He might as well have suggested going to the moon.

'I trust you, *doktor*,' she said simply. 'You will bring my grandson back to me when the time comes.' She smiled at the pretty young nurse by his side and then bent to pick up the offended cat to resume her stroking. He was her only creature comfort now that her grandson was over the water. But he would return . . . of that she was sure.

They took their leave and walked silently back through the village. Anna was worrying about Magdi's chances of survival. It would be terrible to shatter that sort of blind trust.

'Do you think Magdi has a chance?' she asked when they were out of earshot.

'More than a chance,' Simon snapped back. 'Otherwise I wouldn't have built up her hopes, would I? You don't know me very well, do you?'

She bit back her reply. Well enough to know that there's a great deal below the surface, she thought. And whatever it is that's troubling you, I don't want to know. I've got my own problems.

He was pausing beside one of the little houses to talk to a young mother, her children gathered about her skirts. Anna paused to listen.

'I want you to come into hospital before your baby is born,' he was saying firmly. 'I explained why, when I saw you last week. Your mother has agreed to look after the other children . . .'

'But the other *doktor* said I can stay here. He will look after me!' she cried in a shrill voice.

'What other *doktor*?' he asked, with ominous calm.

'He lives in the mountains—up there.' The young woman waved her arm in the general direction of the jungle-clad mountainside.

'Can you describe him to me?'

Anna was surprised at the intensity of his tone. The young mother looked frightened as she gave her description in a quiet, shaky voice.

'He is tall—*very* tall . . . even taller than you, *doktor*. And there is a deep scar on his cheek . . .'

'Thank you,' breathed the doctor, his blue eyes gleaming. 'You've been very helpful. I'll see you next week about coming into hospital. Believe me, it's absolutely essential.'

I'm sure it's Doktor Smith, he was thinking excitedly. The description tallied with the one given him at Kedang hospital. He had wondered if he might find him on Desaman when Magdi's grandmother spoke of the harmful advice given to her by a *doktor*. She had told him the *doktor* charged a small fee for his services. It may be small, he reflected angrily, but it's enough to keep him alive!

He flashed a grateful smile at his patient and stooped to pat the head of her smallest child, who had reached out to touch the doctor's white shirt.

'*Selamat tinggal*—goodbye,' he said gently.

The children waved as the doctor and nurse went out of sight along the village path. As usual, Anna was several paces behind and she arrived breathless at Mohammed's house. Great preparations were being made for the journey to Penasing. Kandiah's mother was taking no chances; she wanted to be sure that she had all her clothes with her. Her son-in-law was trying to convince her that it wasn't necessary to take the entire wardrobe.

Anna gently intervened, on Simon's instructions. 'We'll miss the tide if we don't get a move on,' he hissed. 'You sort the old lady out and I'll organise a stretcher for Kandiah.'

In less than half an hour they were leaving the shore. Kandiah lay on her improvised stretcher with the baby clasped to her breast. In the haste of departure, there had been no time to feed the little mite. Anna checked that he was sucking properly before moving up on deck to sort the luggage. They seemed to have too many people on board and she wanted to find out who they all were.

It transpired that the fisherman who owned the boat had decided to take all his family with him for a trip to the mainland. His two sons, in their best clothes, were charging up and down the deck, unconcerned about the noise of their shoes on the roof of Kandiah's cabin.

'*Sila duduk*—please sit down,' Anna said firmly, and after a moment's hesitation, the boys complied.

They glanced at their mother who was sheltering from the heat of the morning sun, clutching her youngest child, and she nodded her agreement. Anna looked at the mother and thought that at first glance she could be mistaken for a nun. Her head was covered by a white cloth which only revealed her face. Every wisp of hair was hidden and her body was completely covered in a dark blue sarong. Tiny shoes were poking out from under the garment's hem, but there was nothing to indicate whether or not she had ankles. By comparison, Anna's short-sleeved white dress seemed positively daring!

She stretched out her legs on the deck. The brown suntan was turning yellow. It would be wonderful to have the time to lie on a beach in the sun, she thought wistfully; to run into the sea and swim . . . with a romantic companion . . .

Her eyes strayed towards where Simon was talking to the fisherman and his inevitable brother. His fair good looks contrasted vividly with the dark, weatherbeaten, careworn appearance of the Malay men. He's probably older than them, she figured, but he seems much younger. I wonder how old he is—thirty-five, perhaps? But he's had a much easier life than they have . . .

'How's Kandiah?' It was almost as if he had sensed her eyes upon him when he turned to look at her.

'She's feeding at the moment—no problems there,' Anna answered confidently. She was glad they were surrounded by people; it would have been a strain to make this journey alone with Simon and the patient.

They reached Penasing in the afternoon and an *ambulan* was waiting for them on the quayside. The tiny vehicle was crowded as Anna sat in the back with Kandiah, her mother, the baby and Simon. She held the baby tightly as they made the sharp bend into the hospital and then there was a screech of brakes as they pulled up outside Casualty.

Suddenly Simon reached across and taking the baby from her, he said, 'I'm sorry about that day in the rain.'

She smiled up into the blue eyes. Apologies

weren't his style, as a rule! 'I forgive you,' she said quietly.

The ambulance men were already opening the doors to let them out.

'I'd like to do something as a penance,' he continued with a wide grin. 'Would you let me take a look at your mother-in-law some time . . . I mean, a second opinion couldn't hurt, could it?'

Anna wasn't in the least taken in by his uncharacteristic approach, but she was moved by his concern. Perhaps she shouldn't have snapped his head off last night, when he was questioning her. Maybe he was genuinely interested in the case?

'If you think it would do any good,' she replied warily. 'But I warn you, she's a very difficult woman.'

'I've dealt with a lot of difficult women in my time,' he smiled. 'If you can persuade her to come here for an examination, I'll do the rest.'

'Well, I'll try,' she said doubtfully, as she stepped down on to the hot driveway.

Simon followed and handed back the baby. 'Take the little one to your ward for the moment until I've admitted Kandiah.'

It was evening before she saw him again. The afternoon had flown by as she settled in to the ward routine, picking up from where she left off. She decided that these trips away from hospital were highly disturbing in more ways than one! When she met him in the corridor as she went off duty, she was feeling exhausted. They walked towards the main entrance together, and Anna noticed that Simon, for once, was adapting his step to hers.

'Tired?' he asked casually.

She nodded. 'It's been a long day. How's

Kandiah and the baby?' She had sent Nurse Wong to Obstetrics with the infant, so she hadn't seen her patient since she left the ambulance.

'She's fine—and her mother loves playing at nurses! When I left her just now, she was helping to give a bottle feed to our little prem!'

Anna laughed. 'You'll have to put her on the pay-roll!'

Simon stopped short in the middle of the corridor and putting his hands on her shoulders, spun her to face him.

'That's better,' he said softly. 'You should laugh more often.'

She stared up into the expressive blue eyes. 'Such concern, doctor,' she murmured mockingly. 'Twice in one day I find you concerned about my welfare.'

'I like to look after my staff,' he replied evenly. 'Are you off duty now?' His words seemed like an impulsive afterthought.

'Yes, thank goodness. I'm going home to bed.' She began to move away from him, but he caught her arm.

'That seems like a terrible waste of an evening. How old are you, Anna?' he asked gently.

'Twenty-seven—why?'

'Twenty-seven,' he repeated softly. 'You shouldn't spend all your time working or sleeping. These are the best years of your life. You mustn't waste them.'

They had reached the double doors at the entrance to Casualty. Anna was aware that Sister Kasim was watching from her desk.

'I've told you the circumstances of my home life,' she said with a quiet weariness. 'There's nothing I can do about it . . .'

'We'll see about that,' muttered Simon decisively then, raising his voice, he called across to the eavesdropping Sister, 'Sister Kasim, will you ring Nurse Gabell's home and tell them she'll be late. Something important has just come up.'

'Of course, sir,' came back the dutiful reply.

Anna found herself propelled out of the building, and before she could protest they were heading for the car park.

'Are we off on some secret mission?' she asked when she found her voice.

'No, it's not secret. I'm taking you away from hospital, away from patients, and away from demanding old matriarchs. Leave your car here. We'll take mine—don't worry, I'll bring you back.'

She climbed into the blue Daimler, feeling too tired to argue. For once it was nice to be taken care of. She only hoped Safiah would understand when she got the phone call.

The car was gliding up the hill towards the mosque. When they came to the bend in the road Simon took the left-hand fork.

'You're taking me to your father's house, aren't you?' Anna's voice betrayed the nervousness she felt on approaching the huge stone building at the summit of the hill.

'So you've been checking up on me, have you?' he smiled. 'And it was going to be a surprise. How did you know where I live?'

'Everyone knows it. I understand your family is regarded as the aristocracy of the colonial era,' Anna replied quickly.

He noted the edge in her voice. 'Everything's changed since Independence,' he said evenly.

'Most things for the better, I might add. We're getting major advances in medical services . . .' He stopped in mid-sentence, remembering that this was to be a social visit. He mustn't get on his hobbyhorse.

They drove through the wide gates and up the sweeping drive to the front entrance. Four wide columns supported a stone portico in front of the open doors, and from the spacious interior came the sound of music and laughter.

'I think we have guests,' said Simon, as he pulled the car to a halt.

Anna felt a rising panic. Her white dress was no longer white; she had worn it all day. It wasn't fair of Simon to expect her to be seen like this, in such a dishevelled appearance.

'I can't go in looking as if I've been dragged through . . .'

'Yes, you can,' he interrupted in a masterly tone that brooked no contradiction. 'Coral will help you out.'

Anna opened her mouth to ask who Coral was, but there was no need to utter a sound. A tall elegant figure was emerging through the wide front doors, her lips parted in a tinkling of vivacious laughter.

'Simon darling!' The vision had reached inside the car, practically dragging its owner to his feet.

Simon's eyes were shining with admiration as he gazed down at the attractive woman. 'Coral, you look fabulous—as always . . . Oh, there's a friend I want you to meet.' Anna imagined a tone of reluctance crept into his voice as he turned back to watch her extricating herself from the car. 'This is Anna —she's a staff nurse at Penasing.' He lowered his voice. 'Can you fix her up with a change of clothing? She's been working since the crack of dawn . . .'

'Of course!' gushed the vision. 'Come this way, my dear. You must be exhausted.'

Anna felt herself being swept along on a tide of expensive perfume like a piece of flotsam. Simon disappeared into the interior of the groundfloor as the overpowering Coral led her up a grand staircase and flung open a highly polished wooden door.

'Would you like a shower or a bath?—yes, of course you would. Use my bathroom and then take your pick of my wardrobe. This is the cocktails section . . .' She slid back the doors of a cupboard which ran the length of the enormous room. 'This black little number might suit you.'

Anna stood rigid with embarrassment as a flimsy chiffon creation was held against her.

'No, that won't do at all—much too long. You're shorter than I am . . . how about this cream silk? Yes, that suits you—brings out the dark colour of your skin and hair. What do you think? Do you like it, Anna?'

Yes, she liked it, but she wished she could stem the endless patter. Dutifully she smiled, nodded and said she was most grateful.

'Take your time. I'll be downstairs—got to look after our guests,' Coral explained as she crossed back to the door, her high heels making no sound on the thick pile of the carpet.

The door closed and she was gone. Anna breathed a sigh of relief, but at the same time she wished she hadn't come. She had noticed the possessive 'our guests' and wondered where the tall elegant blonde woman fitted into the household.

She might be Simon's sister, she thought hopefully . . . but somehow she didn't think so. Although they were both fairish, she had the feeling that Coral's colour was out of a bottle!

Now I'm being bitchy, she told herself as she stepped into the elegant white bath. The water began to soothe away her worries. What did it matter who the mysterious Coral was!

When she stepped into the cream silk cocktail gown she felt like a new woman. She took her hairbrush out and brushed her shoulder-length hair until it shone. As she was about to return it to her bag, she caught sight of her golden necklace in its tiny polythene bag. She had taken to carrying Simon's present with her everywhere. Safiah had a habit of snooping in her room while she was out, and the last thing she wanted to do was explain about a golden orchid on a chain!

I wonder if I dare wear it? she thought. She held the necklace against her. It nestled at her throat and she decided it set the dress off beautifully. Anyway, Simon would never notice what she looked like, with an elegant creature like Coral around.

Anna felt nervous as she negotiated the wide staircase. The sound of laughter was coming from a large room leading off from the main hall. As she made her entrance, every eye seemed to be upon her.

Simon was the first to speak. 'What a transformation!' He crossed the high-ceilinged room in easy strides and took her arm. 'Come and be introduced . . . You remember Ralph, don't you, from Singapore.'

'Of course.' She smiled up into the kind eyes of

the famous surgeon. 'How's our little patient?' she asked quickly.

Before he could answer, Coral had intervened. 'Now, you promised not to talk shop tonight!' she admonished, shaking an immaculately manicured finger.

'I know, but this is different,' the surgeon answered, turning back towards Anna. 'As I was telling Simon just now, Magdi is making a remarkable recovery. He's undergoing a course of radiotherapy at the moment. I hope to let you people have him back sooner than we thought.'

'Well, that will be financially most acceptable, because this little patient is costing a fortune . . .'

'Coral!' snapped Simon. 'How can you be so mercenary?'

Ralph James pretended not to hear as he took Anna's arm and guided her across the floor towards the open windows. 'Such a beautiful old house, don't you think, my dear?'

She smiled as she tried to concentrate on the beautiful moonlit view. 'Yes, it's lovely,' she agreed quietly.

'In the daytime, you can see the islands on the horizon—Desaman and Tawa—have you been there?' he asked, in a kindly tone.

'I was on Desaman this morning . . . what a long day it's been!' Anna laughed. 'It seems as if I've been awake for a week. But I've never been to Tawa.'

'Oh, but you must come with us tomorrow! Simon!' Ralph raised his voice above the chatter. 'I hear you've never taken Anna to Tawa.'

'Haven't had time.' Simon strode across the room, leaving a disgruntled Coral to supervise the white-coated stewards. He stared down at the newly elegant nurse. 'Are you free tomorrow? . . . no, let me re-phrase that. Are you on duty?'

He had sensed that her initial reaction would be to point out all the work she had to do at home.

'I'm not on duty now until Sunday afternoon,' she began cautiously.

'Fine; you can join the party on Tawa. We have a house there—plenty of room for one extra. Ah, here's Father . . . Another guest for Saturday. This is Anna Gabell; she's helping me with the islands project.'

'I remember you told me about her,' said the tall, older version of Simon. 'How do you do, my dear.'

Anna looked up into the expressive blue eyes and thought how incredibly handsome the man was, for someone of his age. He must be at least . . . she began to do mental arithmetic . . . if Simon was thirty-five . . .

'But you haven't got a drink!' The older man snapped his fingers and one of the stewards hurried over.

'Yes, Sir Lawrence?' He gave a slight bow towards his master.

'Some champagne for the lady.'

A glass was placed in Anna's hand within seconds and she took a sip of the heady bubbles. She had no idea Simon's father was a 'sir'. As she was wondering what he had been knighted for, she noticed a familiar figure crossing the room.

'Do you remember Fay Curtis, my Theatre Sister?' Ralph James asked her.

'Yes, of course. But you look different out of uniform,' Anna replied.

'So do you,' returned Sister Curtis, eyeing

the expensive gown with a mixture of envy and admiration.

'Dinner is served, Sir Lawrence,' announced one of the stewards.

Anna put her glass down on a low, ornately carved table. The champagne had gone to her head. She smiled conspiratorially at Fay Curtis. 'I borrowed the dress from Coral,' she whispered, as they made their way towards the dining room. 'I arrived in a filthy uniform and she took pity on me.'

The Sister smiled back. 'I wondered if that was the case—actually, I've seen her wearing that dress —but don't let it spoil your evening,' she added hastily.

'I won't,' Anna replied firmly, as she gazed round the opulent dining room. But it would be nice to know who Coral actually was.

The table was set for eleven. Anna decided her unexpected arrival must have necessitated a hurried consultation about where she should be placed, and she was relieved to find herself between Simon and Ralph. The older surgeon held her chair as she sat down.

'This is Anna Gabell, who's helping Simon with the islands project,' Sir Lawrence announced from the head of the table.

All eyes were turned upon her from the sea of unknown faces as she was introduced to everyone in turn. She nodded and smiled, trying to remember all the names. There was a Malay government official and his wife, a Chinese consultant from Kedang hospital and a retired English couple who had been living in Penasing since the colonial days. She noticed that Coral was seated at the bottom of the table and was very much in charge of the service at the table. A barely imperceptible movement of her finger was enough to send a steward scurrying to the kitchen to start the next course.

They started with huge Sambal prawns and then proceeded to the main course of chicken with ginger, black mushrooms and rice, followed by melon and papaya for dessert. Anna's weariness disappeared as she appeased her hunger and she began to mellow towards her boss.

The conversation was light and deliberately free of medical gossip, apart from a brief interlude when the Chinese consultant from Kedang spoke suddenly to Ralph James across the table.

'Did you hear about our terrible scandal at the hospital?' he asked earnestly. 'Apparently we've been employing an unqualified doctor since the end of the second world war.'

The room became quiet as all eyes focused upon Mr Kwan.

'I believe something filtered through on the grapevine,' replied Ralph. 'What was the fellow's name?'

'Smith,' Simon supplied without hesitation. 'The man's a menace to the community and should never have been allowed to practise in the first place.'

Anna shivered at his ominous tone and looking sideways saw that he was clenching and unclenching his fists.

'I'm sure my son doesn't mean to pass a slur on the contemporary management at Kedang,' Sir Lawrence put in hastily. 'He's too young to remember the dark days after the war when everything was in turmoil and anyone with a smattering of knowledge about first aid was most welcome.'

'His credentials should have been checked over

the years,' continued his son obstinately. 'This could never happen in the UK.'

'I'm sure it couldn't,' agreed Mr Kwan politely without a flicker of emotion passing over his inscrutable Oriental features. 'But, as you English say, it is all water under the bridge. The police have the matter well in hand. They will find the impostor and bring him to justice.'

'They seem to be taking their time,' said Simon drily. 'Criminal negligence doesn't appear to be a priority issue . . .'

'How do you find conditions now at Kedang, Mr Kwan?' interrupted Ralph hastily. 'I hear you have an excellent new orthopaedic wing.'

The Chinese consultant smiled gratefully. 'It is indeed a model of perfection, and we are very proud of it. We have been forced to expand . . .'

Anna listened to Mr Kwan warming to his subject, not daring to look at Simon. She could hear that he was taking in deep breaths as if to calm himself. He obviously feels very strongly about the Doktor Smith scandal, she thought, but he's decided that the dinner table is not the place to argue it out. She finished her dessert before she dared to turn and face him. To her relief she saw that he had regained his composure.

'Thanks, Simon,' she whispered. 'I enjoyed that —hadn't realised how hungry I was.'

He laughed. 'Better than our supper last night, eh?'

'The service is more sophisticated, isn't it? I wouldn't like to have to use my fingers at this table.' She smiled up into the blue eyes beside her.

'But it's not so romantic—all these people . . .'

'Ssh!' She turned to see if Ralph had heard, but

he was deeply engrossed in conversation with Fay.

Simon bent his head towards Anna so that only she could hear. 'And we can't see the moon over-head.' He was standing up. 'Let's take coffee on the verandah, Father,' he said in a normal voice, as he looked down the table.

'Oh, but we'll get eaten alive by the mosquitoes . . .' Coral began plaintively, but Simon silenced her.

'Rubbish!' He was grinning cheerfully, but Coral looked furious.

'Light an insecticide coil on the verandah, Musa,' Simon asked one of the stewards before moving Anna's chair back. 'Are you willing to brave the great outdoors for your coffee, nurse?'

'Considering we spent the whole night in a primi-tive hut with no mosquito nets, this will seem the height of civilisation!'

As she walked across the room beside Simon, Anna heard Coral's voice.

'The whole night in a primitive hut?' the blonde repeated. 'How terribly cosy!'

Simon had put an arm around Anna's shoulders and he felt the sudden shiver of apprehension running down her spine.

'Don't worry about Coral,' he whispered as they went out on to the verandah. 'She's only jealous.'

'I gathered that,' Anna replied, sinking down into one of the comfortable cushioned cane chairs. It was almost as if he were trying to make her jealous. She hoped she wasn't being used as a pawn in some emotional tangle . . .

'There, the moon hasn't deserted us; he shines

just as brightly here as on Desaman,' he continued evenly, oblivious to the atmosphere he had created.

The others drifted out and the coffee arrived. When everyone was served, Simon turned to Ralph and said he would like his advice.

'I've got a patient who lost the use of her legs in a car crash three years ago,' he was saying, and Anna froze in dismay, knowing full well he was about to discuss Safiah.

She opened her mouth to remonstrate, but saw the determined look in the eyes of her boss. She reminded herself that it was good of him to take an interest, but to describe Safiah as 'his patient' was going too far. It was very doubtful if the matriarch would agree to an examination, let alone treatment.

'She has remained in a wheelchair, without any treatment, and I propose making my first examination tomorrow morning. If you could spare a few minutes, before we leave for Tawa, I would be grateful for a second opinion,' he continued relentlessly.

'Of course, old boy. Only too willing to oblige. You say she's had no treatment for three years? How very strange! Stuck out in some jungle village I suppose?' queried Ralph.

'No, here in Penasing,' the other surgeon replied, catching Anna's eye.

She was looking daggers at him. 'I must be off,' she said hastily.

'So soon?' asked Sir Lawrence. 'I shall look forward to seeing you tomorrow. My boat will leave the quay about noon.'

'I'll be there, sir. Thank you for your hospitality.'

'I'll run you home,' Simon said firmly, placing a hand under her arm.

She allowed herself to be propelled out of earshot before she demurred. 'If you take me back to the hospital, I can drive my own car.'

'What's the point of that? It's almost as quick for me to drive over the hill as down to the hospital. You can come back in the ambulance with Safiah. I'll arrange for one to pick you up about ten-thirty. Ralph and I can do our examination in hospital and then you can come over to Tawa with us while the ambulance returns your mother-in-law home again.'

Anna didn't feel like arguing with him. When he was set on a course of action he was used to getting his own way. She stepped into the luxurious interior of the blue Daimler clutching the dirty uniform in a bag.

They drove along the brow of the hill past the mosque, its magnificent dome shining in the moonlight, and cruised down the other side to the outskirts of Penasing. She glanced up at the determined profile and took a deep breath.

'It won't be easy, you know,' she began. 'I've suggested medical treatment to Safiah before, and she flatly refused.'

'Well, you must insist; be positive! Don't take no for an answer—I never do!'

'I'm sure you don't, she said wryly.

They had reached the front of the shabby house and she asked him to stop. As he turned off the engine she reached for the door handle, but Simon was too quick for her. His strong arm shot across, pinning her to her seat. He leaned across and brushed his lips lightly across her cheek.

'Good night, Anna,' he murmured. 'And don't worry too much. I'm sure the old dear will agree to . . .'

Suddenly the tenderness of his voice and the nearness of his firm masculine body was too much for her. She collapsed sobbing into his arms, clinging to him as if she would never let him go.

'Hey, what's all this about . . . ?' he began calmly, but his arms tightened around her.

She could feel his long, tapering fingers on the back of her hair, holding her head against his chest. She pulled her head away from him and looked anxiously up into his eyes. He was smiling as he bent down and covered her lips with his. There was the heady aroma of masculine soap and after-shave, so distinctive to Simon, and then the feel of his sensual mouth began to drive her wild with feelings of passion. Her body melted against his in the most wonderful embrace she had ever experienced . . .

She was fast losing all control as she pulled away from him, remembering they were parked right outside the house and Safiah might be looking out over the moonlit garden. She was also alarmed at the depth of her feelings. There was no knowing what might happen if they were ever really alone again . . .

'I must go in,' she said breathlessly, smoothing down her hair as she reached for the door-handle.

This time Simon let her go. She turned, once, in the moonlight as she opened the gate, but his eyes were on the road. She let herself in quietly, ashamed that she had given in to a moment of weakness but throbbing with the unsatisfied craving that Simon's lips had aroused.

CHAPTER SIX

'DON'T be stupid! Of course you can persuade her!' Simon's irate voice at the other end of the telephone drove Anna's depression to an all-time low.

'I warned you she was difficult!' Her voice sounded shrill and hopeless, even to her own ears. How could she explain that she had wheedled, cajoled, even promised extra housekeeping money, but her mother-in-law was adamant. She was not going to allow herself to be hospitalised.

'Terrible places, hospitals!' Safiah had flung at her, at the end of their long discussion. 'Ibrahim's father died in one and . . .'

The old lady chuntered on, recounting the number of people she had known who had died in hospital. Anna had wanted to point out that they were all old or terminally ill, and they had merely ended their days more peacefully than they would have done if left untreated. But there was no point in arguing. Safiah could be more stubborn than Simon, and that was saying something, she thought, as she listened now to his furious tone.

'I'm very disappointed in you, Anna,' he was saying. 'And heaven knows what I'm going to tell Ralph James. Does she realise how difficult it is to have a consultation with someone of his calibre up here? Of course she doesn't! If you'd explained it properly . . .'

The line went dead. Anna decided that Simon was too annoyed to continue. She replaced the phone on its cradle. Well, that was the end of that!

'Do you need a lift? I'm going into Penasing.' Razali's gentle tones calmed her agitated thoughts.

She hesitated before replying. What happens now about the Tawa house-party? she wondered. Will I be persona non grata? But it was Ralph who requested that I go along, and it's Sir Lawrence's party, not Simon's . . . and I don't fancy spending the rest of Saturday with Safiah!

'Yes, I'm going over to Tawa with some friends, as a matter of fact,' she replied casually. 'So if you could drop me somewhere near the quay, that would be a great help. I'll be ready as soon as I've briefed Zaleha. Take care of Safiah this evening, Razali. She's not speaking to me.'

Her brother-in-law laughed. 'I don't know why you put up with her tantrums, Anna.'

'Neither do I,' she replied a trifle shortly as she made for the kitchen.

Half an hour later, Razali's old jalopy chugged its way to the end of the road. They rounded the corner, out of sight of the opulent blue Daimler that was arriving in front of the house from the other direction.

Simon turned off the engine and got out, wondering what to say to Anna. He walked away from the house for a while as he tried to gather his thoughts. It had been rude to put the phone down on the girl, but on the other hand, he would have thought she could have persuaded her mother-in-law. It was part of a nurse's training to learn how to handle recalcitrant patients, he reminded himself, justifiably, as he sat down on a seat at the end of the road.

He gazed out to sea, towards the outline of

Tawa. A few hours of swimming and relaxation on those soft white sands would work wonders! he thought. I won't mention the interrupted phone call . . . I'll just turn up and say I thought she'd need a lift, now that the ambulance had been cancelled and her car is at the hospital. He rose decisively and strode back down the road. As he reached Anna's house he paused, stepping back into the shade of a palm tree as he watched the intriguing sight.

An old Malay woman was walking in the garden. She paused by a patch of lilies, gathered several of the blooms and then returned to climb easily into a wheelchair, still clutching her flowers. Then she gave a loud imperious cry.

'Zaleha!'

Her nursing attendant came out of the house to take the flowers inside, and the old woman followed her in the wheelchair.

Simon drew in a ragged breath. So that was it! He wondered how many people knew that Safiah could walk, and why it was being kept a secret. Surely Anna couldn't be part of this hopeless charade . . . or could she? He would soon find out!

He walked purposefully up to the front door.

'*Selamat pagi*,' Zaleha said to the stranger, as she opened the door. She could see his car, but she hadn't heard him drive up. And Safiah has just been out in the garden, she thought in dismay.

'*Selamat pagi*—good morning,' the doctor replied. 'May I speak to your mistress?'

'*Sila masuk*—please come in.' Zaleha led the way to the kitchen, calling in rapid Malay to tell Safiah that she was bringing a visitor.

The old lady was crouched in her chair, her legs

covered by a cotton blanket. She gazed at Simon with open hostility.

'*Siapa nama anda?*' she snapped.

Simon dutifully told her he was Doktor Sinclair from Penasing hospital.

'I don't want to see you,' she retorted angrily. 'I told my daughter-in-law . . .'

'May I speak to your daughter-in-law?' he interrupted equably.

'She has gone away until tomorrow,' the old lady answered, 'leaving me all alone with Zaleha to manage as best I can. That is the sort of undutiful girl my dear son married.'

'She treats you badly, then?' he probed quickly, in a sympathetic voice.

'Sometimes,' the matriarch replied warily. 'Sometimes she goes away for days, and Zaleha does not feed me properly.'

'How dreadful for you!' He crossed the room and took the wizened old hand in his as he scrutinised the wrinkled face.

The old lady stiffened but didn't try to remove her hand. 'Why have you come?' she asked warily.

'I want to help you,' was his truthful reply. 'But first you must tell me about your legs. How long is it since you were able to walk?'

Safiah shrugged and looked away from the piercing blue eyes. 'I don't remember,' she mumbled. 'About three years, I suppose. Since before my son was killed. We were driving through the jungle . . . the road was wet and slippery . . . oil on the surface . . .' She broke off and stared up at him quizzically. 'Why do you need to know all this?'

'Keep going,' said Simon gently. 'It will help me to decide on your treatment.'

'But I don't want treatment,' she began, but the look in his eyes silenced her. There was something about this doctor that appealed to her. He was firm yet kind. It was a long time since anyone had taken the trouble to listen to her—really listen . . .

'There was no moon that night—only black darkness and sheets of rain against the windscreen. The wipers packed up and Ibrahim couldn't see. I told him to stop, but he just kept on. He wanted to get home to Anna . . .'

Simon hardly dared to breathe. It was as if he had put a spell on the old lady as she recounted her tale.

'And then there were big headlights as we rounded a bend. They were coming straight for us . . . Ibrahim swerved, but the lorry hit us!' Safiah gave a strangled sob and Simon squeezed her hand.

Safiah gave an answering squeeze, in recognition of her trust. 'Then I woke up in hospital at Kedang and my legs wouldn't move, *doktor*.'

'I see,' he said in a sympathetic tone. 'Would you like me to come again? We could talk some more. I may not be able to cure you all at once, but simply talking about it might help.'

The old lady frowned. 'If you like—but you must telephone first. I don't like uninvited visitors.'

'I'm a very busy man. Perhaps we should make an appointment,' he replied, taking a chance that she would play it his way. There was a limit to the amount of time he could give to this case. 'I could arrange for an ambulance to bring you to hospital . . .'

'No hospital!' she stated bluntly. 'Zaleha! Show the *doktor* out . . .'

'Then I will come here on Monday afternoon, at three o'clock,' Simon put in quickly, unwilling to destroy the trust he had built up.

'That will be convenient, *doktor*,' Safiah consented in a weary voice. 'Now, leave me. I am tired.'

'*Selamat tinggal*—goodbye.' He followed Zaleha out to the door. The nursing attendant watched until the car drove off before she went back inside to quiz her mistress.

Simon drove thoughtfully through Penasing and out to the quayside. His father's guests were assembling themselves and their luggage on board their boat. There was no sign of Anna. Perhaps she had decided not to come? He wouldn't blame her . . .

Even as he thought this, he heard the sound of the ancient relic of a car grinding to a halt, somewhere near him in the car park, and smiled to himself as he extricated his long legs from the blue limousine.

Anna glanced across at the tall, handsome figure, wondering why he was looking so pleased with himself. She also wondered what sort of a reception he was going to give her. Best to play it cool, she decided.

'Goodbye, Razali. Thank you so much for the lift.' She dropped a dutiful kiss on her brother-in-law's cheek before he crashed into first gear and drove noisily off.

'Anna!' called Simon, above the noise. 'So glad you could come.'

They met in the middle of the car park. He insisted on carrying her weekend bag. Neither of them mentioned their earlier disagreement. The

were like polite strangers as he helped her on
board.

Coral greeted Anna amicably, instructing a
steward to put her luggage in the cabin and
bring another glass. A champagne cork popped and
Sir Lawrence appeared from down below. He
was wearing a jaunty yachting cap, blue sneakers,
cotton drill trousers and an open-necked shirt.
Only the shock of grey hair over his forehead gave
an indication of his age.

'Here you are, my dear . . . hold the glass
steady . . . And how about you, Coral?' He moved
on. 'Ready for a top-up?'

'I find it difficult to believe he's your father,'
Anna whispered to Simon.

He grinned. 'You mean, I look so old and he
seems so young?'

'You know that's not the case,' she smiled. She
was sure he knew himself to be very handsome by
the assured way he moved around and the devastating effect he had on women . . . some women more
than others!

She swallowed hard, remembering how she had
melted in his arms last night. That sort of response
was much too dangerous for her. She mustn't let it
happen again . . .

They were leaving Penasing in a swirl of high-
powered engines. The water was cut in two behind
them, as they made for the open sea. Anna sat near
the bow, gazing out over the blue water towards the
islands in the distance. Fay Curtis came forward
to sit beside her. It was like a continuation of
yesterday evening's dinner party.

Anna smiled at the Theatre Sister, who had
already stripped down to a bikini. 'Nice to get away

from hospital, isn't it?'

Fay returned her smile as she stretched out in the sun. 'You can say that again! You should have stayed on last night. The party had only just begun when you left.'

'I had to get back—family commitments,' Anna said quickly.

Fay glanced at the gold band on Anna's wedding finger. 'You're married, I see. Do you have children?'

Anna shook her head. Why did people always ask if she had children? Was it the accepted thing? Wouldn't it be possible to marry even if you couldn't have children? she asked herself, and her answer was always the same.

'I'm a widow,' she replied quietly. 'And we didn't have children.'

'I'm sorry.' Fay's voice echoed with sympathy.

Is she sorry about me being a widow or having no children? Anna wondered. Both, I suppose. The only thing is, I could find another husband, but I could never have children, so it wouldn't be fair. She had told herself so often over the last three years that she didn't mind spending the rest of her life without a man. And it hadn't seemed to matter until now . . .

'I suppose it's some comfort having a career, isn't it?' Fay observed gently.

'Oh yes, of course. I love nursing.'

'So do I,' agreed the Theatre Sister enthusiastically. 'And Ralph is such a dear. We have a lot of fun—both on and off duty!' she added.

'How long have you . . . er . . . known Ralph?' asked Anna.

'Ages . . . ever since he came out to Singapore.

years ago, with his wife. She died last year. I've always fancied him.'

Anna glanced at her companion, surprised by her candour. It must be the champagne talking, she thought, and glanced round to see if anyone else was listening. But everyone was wrapped up in their own little group, and the noise of the engines, the waves and the chattering drowned everything.

'I don't think he's fully got over his wife's death,' Sister Curtis continued, warming to her subject as she took another sip of champagne. 'But I'm working on him. I know he likes me . . . it's only a question of time. Not that I'd give up work, of course. Oh no; if he popped the question, I'd accept like a shot, but I'd keep on nursing.'

'Wouldn't you stop if you started a family?' asked Anna tentatively.

'We wouldn't start a family!' laughed Fay. 'Ralph has a grown-up family of his own and I'm sure he wouldn't want to start again. You don't need children of your own to make a marriage work, you know.'

'Don't you think so?'

Fay looked up at the earnest sound of Anna's question, thinking the girl seemed to have some kind of hang-up about the subject. 'I've known a lot of very happy childless marriages,' she said, 'and a lot of very unhappy marriages with children. It's the couple who matter, not the number of children.'

'I suppose so . . . But don't you think most men want to have at least one child?' Anna pursued.

Fay shrugged. 'Some do—some don't . . . That's Tawa, over there!' As she pointed out the tropical island with its impressive skyline of trees, she hoped Anna would drop the subject of marriage and children.

'What are you two whispering about?' Simon stood in front of them, waving a champagne bottle.

'Men!' said Fay, with a wicked grin. 'No, thanks; I'd better not have any more champagne. The last glass went right to my head.'

Simon smiled and turned towards Anna, who said she felt the same as Fay. He sat down on the seat beside her as he recharged his own glass.

'I called for you this morning, but you'd gone,' he said, in a matter-of-fact tone.

She looked at him in surprise. 'Did you see Safiah?'

'Yes,' he replied cautiously. 'And she's agreed to begin treatment on Monday.'

'I don't believe it!'

'But I have to go to your house—she won't go to hospital,' he continued, enjoying her look of amazement.

'Even so, it's a step in the right direction.'

'A step in the right direction,' he repeated softly. 'What an apt description!'

She looked puzzled, but he didn't enlighten her. Again Simon found himself wondering if she was in on the secret. He was determined to find out.

As the shoreline of Tawa drew nearer, Anna caught her breath. 'It's beautiful!' she breathed as she took in the white sand shining in the midday sun, the transparent blue sea and the spectacular coral reefs.

'There's the house!' Simon told her, pointing to a group of wooden buildings among the palm trees. 'My father built the main house when I was a child.

He kept on adding to it over the years. But it's stayed the same since Mother died.'

She heard the catch in his voice, but didn't enquire; it was obviously a sensitive subject. They were pulling into the long wooden jetty and a steward helped her to climb up the steep ladder to the platform. Near the shore there was not a breath of air.

'How about a swim before lunch?' Sir Lawrence was stripping off his shirt as he hurried along the jetty to the beach. He dropped his clothes on the soft white sand and, wearing only a small pair of black trunks, he dived in. Most of the guests, anticipating their host's love of swimming, were quick to divest themselves and join him in the water.

As Anna plunged in from a coral-strewn rock, she felt the soothing rush of the clear water on her hot skin. Simon was swimming nearby, and he reached out to touch a strand of her wet hair.

'I'm glad you came, Anna,' he said, smiling at her across the glistening surface of the water.

'So am I,' she replied, feeling as if all her cares had been washed away in the tropical sea.

'Race you back to the shore!' he called.

She turned quickly and struck out, but he was there before her, holding out a large white, fluffy towel. She allowed herself to be wrapped up like a child before she discarded the towel and lay down on one of the sun-loungers which the stewards were placing on the sand, in the shade of the palm trees.

'You've got the best of both worlds here,' she remarked to Simon as he flung his long body on to a chair beside her. 'A tropical island with all the comforts of a luxury hotel.'

He laughed. 'It is pretty marvellous. I tend to take it for granted. It's only when we bring people out here that I remember what a unique spot it is.'

'It's paradise!' Anna exclaimed, gazing around her. A brightly-coloured butterfly had alighted on the flower-pattern chintz of her chair and was doing his best to get a response from the lifelike bloom. 'Just look at this beautiful butterfly! He thinks I'm a flower.'

'And why not? A very pretty flower, I would say.' Simon leaned across and kissed her cheek. 'I noticed you were wearing my orchid last night,' he added softly, and he raised himself on one elbow.

Her heart had started to pound again. 'I think it's a lovely necklace,' she said quickly.

'Wear it tonight—for me.' He was scrambling to his feet. 'I'm going to help Coral sort out the luggage.'

Anna watched him running across the sand away from her towards the tall elegant blonde who was standing beside a pile of bags, directing the stewards. Simon put an arm casually round Coral's waist and drew her away towards the main house. Anna looked out across the water, wishing she had more control over her emotions. He must have brought dozens of girls out here, she thought quickly. And I don't suppose they meant any more to him than I do . . .

Lunch was a barbecue on the beach; steaks and lamb chops with huge bowls of green salad. Afterwards there was a siesta for those who wanted to rest from the intense heat. Anna lay on the cool cotton sheet in her room, listening to the gentle lapping of the waves on the shore, only yards away.

As she drifted off to sleep, she decided that here she had found her paradise island . . .

The sun was low in the sky when she awoke. From the sound of voices outside, she gathered that most of the party were in the sea again. She felt hot and sticky as she reached for her bikini. A cool swim was just what she needed.

Running down the beach, she noticed that the sand was still hot from hours of daytime sun. She plunged into the soothing water and struck out towards a large rock in the centre of the bay. As she swam she bent her head into the water to watch the fascinating marine life. A huge rainbow fish was swimming just beneath her, and in the clear depths she could see a mauve sea anemone sitting on the sand like an ornate cushion. Beside it was a golden sea urchin with a large blue eye in the centre. Further along the sea bed long black sea slugs were lying motionless in their sandy camouflage.

'Spectacular, isn't it?'

Anna raised her head at the sound of Simon's voice. He was only inches away from her, treading water as he spoke.

'I've never seen anything like it!' she breathed.

'Be careful of those big black sea urchins. If you get one of their spikes in your foot, it can be very painful,' he warned, smiling across the surface of the water.

She shivered. 'I'm glad we have our own doctor with us.' She started to move away and he followed.

'But I'm off duty, remember?' he called lightly.

'So you wouldn't help me, even if I were stung by something dreadful?' She tried to keep up the bantering tone.

'I might make an exception for you,' he replied

softly, and then struck out towards the shore in a flurry of waves.

She swam leisurely back to the shore and took an extra long time over preparing for dinner. She was feeling delightfully relaxed by the combination of rest and lack of responsibility.

The sun had sunk below the horizon when she emerged again, having showered and put on a cream dress with a full, ankle-length skirt. Simon walked along the main verandah to meet her. She looked up at him and enjoyed the unmistakable admiration in his eyes.

'I'm glad you remembered to wear the orchid.' He reached forward and touched the gold flower at her throat.

Anna remained absolutely still, hardly daring to breathe for fear that he would notice her excited response to his touch.

'Come and have a Tawa Special,' he said, dropping his hands to his side.

She followed him to a table and sat down, wondering what a Tawa Special was.

'This is Paul,' Simon told her, as a tall, dark young steward appeared with a tray of drinks. 'He lives out here permanently and runs the house for my father.'

The handsome Malay gave a wide smile, his white teeth shining in the dark skin. 'Good evening, madame,' he said as he placed two long glasses on the table.

'Paul invented the Tawa Special for us. I can't even begin to remember the ingredients . . .'

'Gin, vodka, Bacardi, Cointreau, lime cordial, angostura bitters and soda, sir,' supplied Paul.

Anna's eyes widened. 'It sounds lethal.' She

ook a tentative sip, while both men watched.
Mmm . . . it tastes good!'

Simon laughed at her reaction and the young
teward went away, looking pleased with himself.

Dinner was served in the cool dining room, open
o the sea on one side. As they dined they could
lear the waves lapping gently on the shore. It was
he same assembled company as the previous evening, but Anna thought how much more relaxed
everyone looked after their day on the island. Only
one of the guests had suffered any ill effects from
he outdoor day, and she had retired to bed. It was
he wife of Sir Lawrence's friend from pre-
ndependence days who had sent her apologies at
peing absent from dinner.

'Bad luck about Daphne,' Sir Lawrence was
aying. 'What exactly is the trouble?'

Daphne's husband, Rodney Squires, a retired
architect, shrugged his shoulders. 'Oh, you know
what these women are like, Lawrence! She never
could stand the climate—even when she was
young. Always had to keep hopping back to the UK
or a breather. More like an excuse for a shopping
spree at Harrods, I always used to think!' He took a
arge drink of wine and looked at his old friend for
noral support.

'Yes, it's hard on the ladies out here,' Sir
Lawrence said quietly. There was a faraway look in
his eyes.

'So it's just the heat, is it?' Simon asked quickly,
before his father could start brooding.

The architect nodded sagely and pulled absent-
mindedly on his white handlebar moustache.

'She's been a bit off colour since she got back two
weeks ago. Always takes her a while to adapt.

Nothing that a good night's sleep won't cure.' He drained his glass and looked round for one of the stewards to top him up.

'Well, let me know if there's anything I can do,' Simon said firmly. Rodney Squires was not one of his favourite people, but he thought the world of Daphne.

She had been one of his mother's friends and his main source of comfort during Elizabeth Sinclair's terminal illness. It it hadn't been for Daphne, he would have felt terribly lonely when his mother died. He was only seven at the time and was quickly packed off to school in England, but there were the holidays to contend with. Daphne had somehow managed to fill the gap left by his mother. She had even found time to visit him at school when she went over to the UK, and he remembered how much her visits had meant to him, especially when all the other boys had mothers.

Anna could hear the compassion in his voice when he enquired about Daphne Squires, and her heart went out to him. He's a born doctor, she thought. I'd love to be treated by him. She ate some of her grilled fish. It tasted quite delicious, but she wasn't hungry. She was terribly conscious of Simon's arm, almost touching her own.

The stewards cleared away the main course and brought bowls of fresh fruit—papaya, melon, bananas and pineapple, all grown on the island. Afterwards there was coffee on the verandah. The talk turned, inevitably, to what they were going to do the next day. Sir Lawrence proposed they sail round to the other side of Tawa for a lunch picnic.

'I'm afraid I have to go back during the morning,

Anna put in. 'So you'd better count me out. I'm on duty at one.'

'I'll take you back to hospital,' Simon told her. 'I've got to get some work done.'

Her heart started to thump madly at the thought of returning over the water alone with him. The guests started to drift off to bed, tired by the sun and sea. Simon stood up to help his father. Anna noticed that everyone was escorted, courteously, to their room. Most of the guests had been assigned to one of the two smaller beach houses, but Simon, his father and Coral slept in the main house. Again she found herself wondering about Coral . . .

'Good night, Anna.' Simon was looking down at her, his facial expression masked by the shadow of the moon, as he stood outside her door. He took the gold orchid in his fingers and she waited, motionless, for his kiss.

But he turned away suddenly and strode purposefully towards the main house. She went inside and closed the door, telling herself she was glad he hadn't kissed her. The sooner they returned to hospital and their professional relationship the better!

Anna was awakened in the middle of the night by the loud screeching of a lizard on the thatched roof. For a moment she couldn't think where she was, and then, as her eyes became accustomed to the moonlight streaming in through the window, she remembered. Restlessly she turned over and gazed up at the mosquito net. She felt hot and there was not a breath of air. The sound of the sea drifted towards her.

I wonder if it's any cooler on the beach, she thought desperately. Maybe if I go for a stroll by the sea, I shall be able to go back to sleep.

Carefully she climbed out of bed, tucking in the mosquito net behind her to ensure an insect-free sleeping space on her return. The beach looked like a stretch of tropical desert, shining white in the moonlight, as she stepped outside her door. Myriads of stars clustered in the sky like tiny diamonds clinging to a dark blue velvet curtain. And yes, it was fresher on the beach!

Her bare feet hardly touched the sand as she ran down to the water's edge. She felt a strong desire to plunge in and go for a swim, but decided that it might be a foolish thing to do on her own. If she got into difficulty in the sea there would be no one to save her. She was quite alone under the stars.

Even as she contemplated her solitude the sound of muffled footsteps came to her ears, and she turned away from the sea and looked up the beach.

At first she thought it was a dream. Simon was coming towards her, looking incredibly handsome in skin-tight black trunks. She could see the sweat on his chest glistening in the pale white light of the moon.

'I couldn't sleep,' he said as he reached her. 'So I'm going for a swim to cool off. Are you coming in?'

For the first time, Anna was aware that she was wearing nothing but a flimsy nightdress. She glanced down at it, and he laughed as if reading her thoughts.

'Take it off, for heaven's sake. The fish won't mind! Besides, it's dark out there on the water.' He plunged in, completely unconcerned at her dilemma.

As she watched his athletic figure streaking away through the waves, she pulled off the nightdress and followed him. After a few seconds he turned and smiled his approval.

'Good girl! Doesn't that feel better?' He was treading water so that she could catch up with him.

'It's wonderful!' she called truthfully. 'Just what I needed. It was impossible to sleep.'

She reached him and felt suddenly very vulnerable with the sea lapping round her bare skin. The unexpected exertion had left her breathless. She moved away and clung to the large rock in the middle of the bay. It still felt warm, even in the middle of the night. And then she saw he was coming towards her . . .

She held on to the rocky surface as if it were her lifeline. Suddenly the sheer madness of the situation hit her forcibly and she began to laugh.

'Hey, what's the joke?' Simon was standing in the water beside her. As he spoke, he hauled himself up on to the rock and held out his hand towards her.

Without thinking, Anna grasped it and allowed herself to be pulled up out of the sea, up on to the bare surface of the rock. She lay on her back, staring up at the stars.

'I was thinking how hilarious it is to be out here in the middle of the night . . .'

'With only the moon and the stars to see us,' he whispered into her ear as he lay down beside her. 'I don't think it's hilarious. I think it's the most natural thing in the world for two people to be together like this.' He bent down and put his lips gently on her cheek.

She turned and looked up into the depths of his

blue eyes. Her face was reflected in the moonlight shining on him.

Suddenly he pulled her roughly against his hard body. She was held in a vice-like grip, but the sensations flooding through her were the most wonderful she had ever experienced. With a low moan she closed her eyes and abandoned herself to the passion that was mounting between them. It was like floating away from the world and all its cares. Her body ceased to exist . . . wave after wave of sensual frenzy swept over her until she cried out at the final moment of ecstasy.

CHAPTER SEVEN

IT MIGHT have been a minute or an hour later. Time had ceased to exist. A voice was calling from the shore.

'Simon! Where are you? Daphne needs your help!'

'I'm here, Father. Wait there!' Simon was instantly on the alert as he plunged into the water and swam back to the shore.

Anna watched until the two men had disappeared into the main house before she slid into the water. As the cooling sea touched her skin she came to her senses. What had she done! Her mind reeled with confused recriminations as she struck out for the shore. She must have been mad! Yes, that was it; she had temporarily gone out of her mind. But as she stepped on to the sandy shore she knew she was back in the real world and would have to face the consequences of her momentary lapse . . .

But it wasn't momentary! She had wanted Simon to make love to her with all her heart. And she had given in to her heart when she should have listened to her head.

She pulled on her nightdress and hurried into her room. Voices were coming from the main house. It sounded like a medical emergency. She would have to go and help.

Minutes later, clad in a sober white cotton dress, she made her way in through the open door of the main house. Lights were on in most of the rooms, but the action was up in Daphne Squires' room. Her husband, Rodney, was pacing the terrace outside looking desperately worried.

'What's the trouble?' she asked him.

'Daphne's doubled up with pain. I've never seen her like this before. Simon's in there with her . . .'

Anna went into the bedroom and, in spite of the grave situation, her legs felt as if they would melt beneath her at the sight of Simon, still in black trunks, bending over his patient. He barely acknowledged her arrival, except to say,

'Go and fetch my bag and draw up morphine, 15mg stat!'

She hurried out of the room. 'Where's Simon's room?' she asked Rodney anxiously.

'It's that one.' He pointed along the terrace.

As she pushed open the door, Coral came out of the next room, looking cross and tired. 'What on earth's going on?' she snapped wearily.

'Daphne's ill—I've come for Simon's bag.'

'Let me help you.' Coral went into the room first.

As Anna followed, she noticed the faint aroma of aftershave and the distinctive soap she had used in their pool on Desaman.

'Here it is. Anything I can do?'

'I don't know until Simon has come up with a diagnosis. Thanks for the bag.' Anna hurried out, not wanting to waste a precious second.

She drew up the morphine, swabbed Daphne's arm and gave the injection. Simon nodded approvingly.

'You'll start to feel less pain soon, Daphne . . . Wipe her face, nurse,' he added quietly, falling easily back into their professional relationship.

Anna rinsed some gauze under the tap and soothed her patient's skin. 'She's very hot,' she whispered.

'I know. We'd better get her back to Penasing. I've asked Paul to get one of the smaller boats ready. It's almost sunrise.' He had turned away from the patient while he was speaking and lowered his voice.

'Have you got a provisional diagnosis?' she asked.

'Renal colic, I think,' he replied quickly. 'The pain is spasmodic, intense and radiating down into the groin and the inner aspect of her left thigh. I would say there's a renal calculus in the ureter. We can do an X-ray back at the hospital and then take it from there. The main thing at the moment is to ease the pain and stop her from panicking. Stay with her while I check on our transport arrangements and ring the hospital to order an ambulance.'

'Shall I wake Ralph and Fay?'

For a moment the glimmer of a smile crossed his face. 'They seem to be the only ones still asleep. No, don't waken them. We can handle this together.'

He turned away abruptly and ran down the stairs. Anna went back to her patient.

'Don't worry, Daphne,' she whispered encouragingly. 'We'll soon have you in hospital.'

'What do you think it is, nurse?' Daphne screwed up her face as another spasm gripped her abdomen.

'It might be a stone in the kidney. We'll X-ray you when we get back to Penasing.'

Daphne nodded her head and took a deep breath to steady herself. 'I feel a bit woozy now,' she mumbled.

'That's the morphine taking effect,' Anna told her.

'Good . . .' The older woman closed her eyes and her breathing became easier.

Simon returned with a stretcher, after a few minutes. As the small procession wended its way down to the jetty, the sun began to peep over the top of the hill, diffusing its warm red light across the sand.

A new day, Anna thought. And I feel like a new person! There was no point in regretting what had happened if it made her feel so alive . . .

They loaded their precious cargo on to the boat and cast off. She sat beside Daphne, ready to reassure her, but mercifully, her patient drifted off to sleep. Looking across, Anna saw that Simon was engrossed in some paperwork he had brought with him. Or perhaps he's avoiding me, she thought anxiously. He wants me to realise that the whole incident was a mistake, that it should never have happened.

She turned her face away from the morning sun towards the Malaysian coastline. I've been such a fool! she told herself vehemently.

There was an ambulance waiting for them on the quayside. The sirens wailed as they drove through Penasing towards the hospital. Sister Kasim, roused from her Sunday morning lie-in, was waiting for them in Casualty. A radiographer was alerted and an X-ray taken.

'As I thought,' breathed Simon as he put the X-rays up on the screen. 'Can you see that dark object here, Anna?'

'Yes; it's a calculus, isn't it?'

'Fortunately it's not impacted in the ureter. We'l

give her an antispasmodic every four hours and step up her fluid intake. With luck the stone may pass down the ureter; it's not very big, as you can see. I want you to check all urinary output. Now, atropine 0.6mg stat and four-hourly.' He made as if he was on his way out.

'Do you want a private room for Daphne?' asked Anna quickly.

'Of course.' He sounded surprised that she should even have asked.

'What do you think was the cause of the renal calculus?' She was totally professional now; her only concern was for the patient.

'Any factor which produces concentration of the urine, such as diminished fluid intake with excessive sweating. She's only just come back from England, so her body may not have had time to adjust. She's post-menopausal, so there could be some decalcification. Alternatively, we might find some parathyroid disease or a urinary infection. We'll have to check all these things out. Start by arranging for a serum calcium level estimation. I'll leave you to settle her in when she wakes up.' Simon was tapping his fingers on the cotton sheet of a nearby examination couch in a display of characteristic impatience.

'Don't let me detain you,' Anna said quietly, as she turned back to her patient.

Moments later she heard him go out, his shoes echoing down the long corridor. She took a deep breath and told herself it was over—over before it began. She had behaved foolishly, but it must never happen again. It had meant nothing to Simon. She was going to put the whole thing out of her mind.

She settled her patient in one of the few private

rooms, gave her some atropine and instructed the
nurse to keep a constant check on intake and
output. Daphne was drowsily grateful to her as she
took her leave, promising to call in before she went
off duty.

Back on Wad Kanak the children greeted her
with their usual delight. Little Hayati was excited at
the prospect of going home that afternoon; her
mother was going to come to collect her and she
was going to see her baby brother again. Anna
listened to the little patient's delight as she
examined the appendicectomy wound.

'That's healed nicely,' she told the girl. 'But
you're not to do too much heavy lifting when you
get home. Let Mummy carry the baby around.'

Hayati nodded but didn't seem to be listening.
Anna decided she would have to have a firm word
with her mother; it was important that the girl had
adequate rest.

When the mother came in she gave her careful
instructions about Hayati, admired the baby
brother and waved goodbye at the door. She felt
sorry to see her go. The appendicectomy had been
the first time she had worked with Simon, she
remembered. He had seemed so distant . . .

She busied herself with the other patients, feeding and settling the ones who had no relatives with
them. It was dark when she went off duty. She
hurried along the corridor to spend a few minutes
with Daphne.

Her patient was sitting up in bed. Simon was
standing beside her smiling down. He turned to
look at Anna.

'See how well she looks! I've just got the results
of the serum calcium test and we can exclude the

possibility of disease of the parathyroid glands.'

'That's good news.' Anna sank down on the counterpane and smiled at Daphne. 'I hope you've been drinking a lot,' she added in a concerned voice.

'Pints and pints of very boring barley water.' Daphne pulled a face and Simon laughed.

'I'll see if we can organise some fruit juice. Sorry I have to forbid alcohol.'

'I don't mind. Thanks for all your help. Why don't you two run along and relax for a while? I'm sure you deserve it after all your hard work,' the older woman said.

There was a moment's pause before Anna spoke hurriedly. 'I have to get back home, so I'll say good night.' She was out of the room before either of them could say anything.

As she hurried down the corridor towards Bilek Kecemasan, she half expected Simon to come after her. She was going to tell him exactly where their relationship stood. When she got nearer to the front door, she knew he wasn't going to, and she told herself it was a relief. But as she climbed into her old car her cheeks were damp, and this time it wasn't the monsoon rain.

She started the engine and steered the car into the driveway.

'Anna!'

Her heart stopped. He was coming after her! She put the brake on and waited. His fair hair was falling over his face as he stooped to look through the driving window.

'Nearly missed you,' he announced breathlessly. 'Tell your mother-in-law to be in at three o'clock tomorrow.'

Her heart sank. That was all he wanted to say, was it? 'She never goes out,' she replied coldly. 'But I'll tell her to be ready.'

She moved her hand to the gear lever, pointedly, and he straightened up, standing at the side of the driveway, a solemn faraway look in his eyes.

'Good night, Anna,' he said, but his voice was drowned in the noise of the engine.

She drove the car more fiercely than usual. She had thrown caution to the winds. Suddenly it didn't seem to matter whether the car lasted for another year or another day. It was such a trivial consideration when her mind seethed with emotional conflict.

It was a relief to find the house in darkness. She crept up to her lonely room and cried herself to sleep. In her dreams, there was a tall, dark, desirable man; every time she came near him he moved further away, and then, at last, she touched him and he crumbled into a thousand pieces of white sand . . .

She woke up in a blind panic to find she was wet through with perspiration. A tiny finger of daylight peeped over the sill, but it was still early. She got up and went down to the poky little shower room off the kitchen. After a cold shower, she felt able to face the world again. No more romantic notions, she told herself harshly as she put the coffee on the ancient stove.

Sister Kasim looked surprised when Anna walked in through the main entrance.

'You're early, Staff Nurse! What's the matter —couldn't you sleep?'

If you only knew, thought Anna as she put on a bright, professional smile. 'Can't wait to ge started,' she replied. 'How's Mrs Squires?'

'She's had a good night. Only one mild attack of renal colic, but it does mean the calculus hasn't yet been passed. We'll finish off all the tests today. Do you want to go in to see her?' asked Sister.

'Is she awake?'

'Oh yes, and she asked if you'd visit her some time today. It might be as well to go now before we get busy.'

Anna made her way to the small private wing. It might be as well to go before Dr Sinclair gets there, she thought as she pushed open the door to Daphne's room.

'Anna! How nice of you to call so early.' The older woman was sitting up in bed reading a magazine.

'You look much better than yesterday,' said Anna, casting an expert eye over the charts before she sat down on the chair at Daphne's bedside. 'What's this? Romantic fiction?'

Daphne laughed. 'I may be over sixty, but I still believe in romance—even if Rodney is a bit of an old stick-in-the-mud . . . Oh dear, I shouldn't have said that, should I? It sounds so disloyal, after all our happy years together.'

'You believe in loyalty in marriage, do you?' Anna asked gently.

'Oh, absolutely! There's no other way to make it work. When you're married, my dear, you'll soon find that out . . .'

'I have been married,' put in Anna quietly. 'I'm a widow.'

'So you'll know what I'm talking about. I'm sorry you're a widow . . .' Daphne paused awkwardly and Anna knew the inevitable remark would follow. '. . . Still, you're still young. You'll find someone else.'

Anna stood up and put on a false smile. The last thing she wanted this morning was a discussion of her love life.

'Coral is a widow too,' the older woman continued, unaware that she had touched a sore spot. 'But she lives in hopes of marriage. I expect he'll marry her one of these days. It's only a question of time before he realises he's in love with her . . .'

Her voice trailed away as the door opened.

'Who's in love with whom?' asked Simon in a cool, distant voice.

Anna's pulses raced as she looked at the morning-fresh surgeon, his stethoscope slung casually over the spotless white open-neck shirt.

'Never you mind!' smiled Daphne. 'You shouldn't eavesdrop when I'm chatting with my nurse. It's women's talk.'

'In that case, you'd better keep quiet while I do my examination. I wouldn't want to hear something that wasn't meant for my ears,' he replied. 'Perhaps you'd help me, Anna?'

Anna hesitated. This wasn't her department. Theoretically she could decline, but she decided not to draw attention to the fact. She started to remove Daphne's pillows and turn back the sheet.

'How are you feeling now, Daphne?' Simon asked as he spread his long fingers across the abdomen, feeling for signs of tension.

'I've had one short attack of pain, otherwise I seem to be improving.'

He nodded. 'We'll finish the tests today. Keep on drinking as much as you can take . . . thank you, nurse,' he added absently.

He doesn't even remember it's me! Anna thought angrily as she replaced the sheet and tidied the bed. 'I must be getting along to my ward,' she said, as she made for the door.

'Oh yes, of course.' At last he seemed to notice her as a person. 'Thank you for your help . . .'

But she was already outside the door, hurrying down the corridor to Wad Kanak.

There was no time to think about him during the long busy day. It was only as she drove away that evening that she remembered he would have been to see her mother-in-law, with a view to starting treatment. She smiled to herself as she wondered what sort of a reception Safiah had given the distinguished surgeon.

'He was very kind and patient,' Safiah volunteered, in answer to her query.

They were sitting out on the back porch after a simple supper of fish soup, rice, and papaya. Razali had offered to do the dishes so that Anna could talk to his mother about the doctor's visit that afternoon.

'Yes, but what did he actually do?' Anna asked impatiently.

'Do?' Safiah looked puzzled at the question. 'Why, he talked to me, of course.'

'You mean to say he didn't even examine you?'

The older woman drew the cotton blanket tighter over her legs. 'Of course not!' she snapped. 'He says he doesn't need to examine me if I don't want him to—and I don't! He told me he can find out what the problem is simply by talking to me.'

'But what did you talk about?' Anna's high-pitched voice gave some indication of her exasperation.

'Oh . . . everything,' the matriarch answered vaguely. 'He told me all about his childhood in the big house on the hill, and I told him all about Ibrahim and Razali . . . and a little bit about you.'

'Sounds fascinating!' Anna's sarcasm was lost on her mother-in-law. 'And did you discuss who's going to pay for this . . . er . . . treatment?'

'He said he would arrange that with you,' Safiah replied. 'I thought you must have come to some sort of an agreement on the subject.'

'No, we haven't . . . but we will,' Anna finished off decisively.

Razali came out on to the porch, drying his hands on a kitchen cloth.

'So the famous *doktor* is going to get you walking, is he?' he asked with a broad smile.

'Maybe he will,' replied his mother quietly.

Anna flashed a warning look at Razali. 'That's enough questions for tonight,' she said quickly. She was furious at the way Simon was handling the case. It was obvious there was no hope, and yet he was encouraging Safiah to be optimistic.

'Tomorrow night I shall be in Singapore,' Razali put in hurriedly. 'I'm going to miss you both.'

'And we shall miss you, son. But Anna will take care of me.'

Anna felt suddenly desperately tired. The long evenings alone with Safiah stretched ahead of her. She would grow old as her mother-in-law and sit outside on the porch, in her widow's weeds, cherishing the memories of her lost youth . . .

'Time for bed!' she announced firmly.

'Not yet,' grumbled Safiah. 'Zaleha will help me. You run along if you're tired. I want to talk to Razali.'

Anna excused herself and went up to her room. She was going to miss Razali, she thought, as she got ready for bed. He had been such a comfort since Ibrahim died. And now she had no one in whom she could confide . . . and no one to share the burden of Safiah's paralysis. Because it seemed certain, from Dr Simon Sinclair's approach, that he wasn't interested in the case. It was just another medical fee for him.

CHAPTER EIGHT

IN THE WEEKS that followed, Anna saw little o
Simon. There were no further medical trips to th
islands for her. He seemed to be concentrating o
setting up the surgical unit at Penasing, but sh
knew that at least on one occasion he had take
one of the nurses from Casualty with him out t
Desaman. On other visits he had taken to goin
alone for the weekly clinics.

She told herself she was relieved . . . it was bette
this way. They could no longer go on workin
together as they had done before that fateful nigl
on Tawa.

And then one day he turned up on Wad Kanak
as if nothing had happened, and asked if her ba
was packed.

Her heart thumped madly at the sight of him. H
looked somehow thinner and very sunburnt, as
he'd been on a long journey into the jungle.

'I've got a change of clothing and my medic
bag, if that's what you mean,' she answere
obliquely.

'Good. They're bringing Magdi back from Sing
pore this afternoon. I thought we could take hi
back this evening and stop over to do some work i
the morning. There are a number of patients I mu
see on the island.' Simon was regarding her with
solemn professional look, tapping his finge
absently on the desk.

'I'll have to phone Safiah,' she put in quickly.

uppose it's all right to leave her while she's under-
oing your treatment, doctor?' She couldn't resist
his last cynical remark. It infuriated her to see her
nother-in-law being taken for a ride. In all the
veeks he had been treating her, Simon had never
nce examined his patient. All he ever seemed to
lo, according to Safiah, was chat, and Anna had
nade a point of being elsewhere when he called.

'Oh yes, there's absolutely no reason why she
an't be left,' he replied evenly. 'Besides, Zaleha is
vith her, isn't she?'

'Of course,' she answered lightly. 'I haven't had a
hance to discuss the question of your fee,' she
idded tentatively.

'Oh, don't worry about that. Wait till we see
ome improvement and then we'll discuss it.' He
eemed anxious to be off.

'So you think there will be some improvement?'
he queried relentlessly, staring up into the blue
:yes.

He shifted his gaze. 'Let's say I'm quietly
:onfident that I can accomplish something, nurse.'

'So it will be payment by results, doctor?' she
napped back at him.

'Something like that. And now, if you'll excuse
ne . . .'

He left her standing by the desk, her eyes sting-
ng with unwelcome tears. Damn the man! How
lared he upset her, just when she thought she was
)ver him!

She made the phone call to Safiah during her
nidday break. Her mother-in-law wasn't pleased,
)ut she brightened up when Anna told her who she
vas going with.

'Such a wonderful *doktor*!' she gushed, with

uncharacteristic feeling. 'I do enjoy his visits. Don't let him work too hard out there—some of those islanders can be very demanding.'

'I'll take care of him, Mother.'

'And remind him about my next treatment, won't you?' Safiah continued anxiously.

Anna assured her that she would. Well, if nothing else comes of it, he's given the old woman a new interest in life, she thought charitably. I only hope she won't be too disappointed when she realises there's no hope.

At the end of the afternoon she reported to Sister Kasim, in Casualty. The Malay Sister was holding a brown baby on her lap, cooing and gurgling at him as if he were her own.

'Magdi!' Anna gasped happily. 'Haven't you grown! Oh, you darling boy!' She took the baby in her arms and he gave a wide smile. 'Look! he's got some teeth!'

'I would hope he has, nurse.' Simon had come into Casualty through the main entrance. 'He's been weaned on to solid food—not before time, I might add.'

'And how's the tumour? she asked anxiously.

'Completely eradicated. Ralph has done a marvellous job and there's no sign of any secondaries.' He was smiling happily as he looked down at the nurse and the little patient.

'That's wonderful!' Anna breathed thankfully.

'The ambulance is waiting for us. Let's go and return him to his grandmother.' He was already moving towards the door.

She followed him, clutching her precious charge.

'I'll carry your bag,' offered Sister Kasim helpfully.

Anna climbed into the *ambulan* and sat down carefully. Simon she noticed, had chosen to sit with the driver. That was fine by her! She told herself that she had no desire to be near him ever again.

The hospital motor launch was waiting for them down on the quayside. It would take longer than going by plane, but Anna was glad she would be spared the ordeal! As the shoreline of Penasing receded, she began to relax. There was something about the open sea that soothed away her tension. She smiled down at the baby in her arms. He looked sleepy. Gently she carried him down into the little cabin and placed him on one of the bunks, arranging a barricade of cushions so that he couldn't fall off.

The sun was dipping down into the sea when she went back on deck. Simon was chatting to the young Malay skipper, but he broke off when he saw Anna and joined her in the stern.

'Is Magdi asleep?' he asked in a cool, professional voice.

'Yes . . . He seems in excellent health, doesn't he?' She almost added the word 'sir'! It was that sort of discussion, as if they were total strangers.

'I saw another of our patients yesterday,' he continued, in the same vein. 'Daphne Squires—you remember her?'

'Of course!' How could she ever forget that night on Tawa! 'Is she recovered?'

'Yes; she's convalescing in our house on Tawa', he replied. 'Coral's looking after her.'

'That's nice for her.' Anna gazed out across the darkening waves. So he was on Tawa yesterday, was he? And Coral too! How convenient! She checked her thoughts quickly. It had nothing to do with her. She mustn't get involved.

'No further recurrence of renal calculi?' she asked brightly.

'None whatsoever. It was a one-off attack brought on by dehydration.'

Anna turned away from him again. It's going to be easy to keep our distance this time, she told herself.

Simon went back to talk to the skipper, and she closed her eyes, swaying gently with the motion of the boat. As the shoreline of Desaman drew nearer she went down into the cabin to get Magdi ready.

There was a small reception party waiting for them on the little narrow jetty. Word had got through that the *doktor* was bringing back his tiny patient. Anna could make out the thin figure of Magdi's grandmother leaning against a wooden pole as she scanned the approaching boat.

'Magdi!' the old lady called, when she saw the baby in the nurse's arms.

There were several minutes of confusion as they disembarked. Magdi was at first unwilling to leave the safety of Anna's grasp, and he started to cry when the grandmother he had forgotten tried to force her attentions on him. Anna had to carry him all the way to their tiny wooden house with the grandmother holding on to him.

He brightened up when he reached his home. It was as if he remembered the few treasured possessions in the small interior. A young girl was waiting inside, smiling shyly at the European nurse.

'This is my niece,' explained Magdi's grandmother. 'She is going to stay with me to help me. Her mother is my youngest sister. She lives nearby.

nd she too will come to give me some help when I
eed it.'

'I'm very glad about that,' said Anna, with relief.
he had been wondering how the old lady was
oing to manage.

'It was your *doktor*'s idea,' the grandmother
ontinued solemnly. 'He went to see my sister and
rranged everything. My niece will be paid for her
ervices. She is a good girl . . .'

The old lady chatted on, her soft Malay voice
vashing over Anna. It was good to see her so
ontent again, she thought, casting a practised eye
ver the little house. There would have to be a few
hanges here, but basically it was adequate and
ery clean. She spent a long time explaining how to
ook after Magdi and stayed to supervise his sup-
er. After making the girl promise to waken her in
he night, if necessary, she walked along the village
ath to the new medical quarters.

This is an improvement, she thought as she
limbed up the wooden steps. It was a large, con-
erted village house on wooden stilts. Inside she
ound a main treatment area, complete with exam-
nation couch. Other rooms led off from here, but
here was no indication of what they were to be
sed for. She opened the first door and stepped
ack hurriedly.

'I'm sorry, Simon, I didn't know this was your
oom,' she gasped.

He was lying on a narrow camp bed, clad only in
 pair of brief shorts. 'That's OK,' he said, raising
imself up off the bed. 'I was waiting for you to get
ere. This is your room, next door.' He opened it
p to reveal a simple bedroom lit by an oil lamp.

An insecticide coil was burning in the corner and

a mosquito net had been tucked into the mattress.

'It's positively civilised!' Anna exclaimed.

'I'm glad you approve. I've fixed up a shower room round the back, so you won't have to bathe in the stream in the morning—unless you want to.'

His eyes seemed to be boring inside her as he stood on the threshold to her room. She was relieved about the shower. She definitely didn't want to share a stream bath with him! That was all in the past.

'Are you hungry?' he asked.

'No. I had some supper with Magdi.' She had accepted a small bowl of rice from the grandmother, thinking it would be easier than sharing a meal with Simon.

'I'll say good night, then.'

Anna heard his door closing, but was glad that the walls were thicker than in the hut they shared last time they were here! At least she wouldn't have to lie awake listening to the sound of his breathing.

The night sounds closed in on her when she extinguished the oil lamp. The gentle noise of the waves lapping on the shore nearby mingled with the drone of the insects, the rhythm pattern disturbed occasionally by the screech of a lizard.

She was up soon after daylight. After a shower in the small hut at the back, she went along to see Magdi and spent an hour instructing the young girl. She helped her to bath him in a large tin basin before returning to the medical house.

Simon was sitting outside on the narrow wooden verandah, wearing cotton slacks and a short sleeved shirt. He always gave Anna the impression that his clothes had been freshly pressed. Sh wondered how he did it. By comparison, she felt hot and dishevelled.

'Come and have some breakfast,' he called nonchalantly.

She negotiated the wooden steps up to the verandah and sat down at the table opposite him.

'How's Magdi?' he asked as he poured her a cup of strong black coffee.

'He's fine, and the girl is learning fast. That was a good idea, to get help for his grandmother,' she added, in a matter-of-fact voice.

'It was the only thing to do. I wouldn't have allowed him to return without this sort of arrangement. His grandmother is very loving, but she's getting too old to have charge of a baby. The girl wants to be a nurse, so I've promised to help her when the time comes.'

'I thought she seemed interested,' said Anna as she helped herself to a bowl of fresh fruit. 'How did you manage to get a wage for her while she's looking after Magdi?'

'Let's just say it was a private arrangement,' Simon replied vaguely.

She looked puzzled but decided not to pursue the subject. There was something else she wanted to discuss.

'While we're talking about money . . .' she began tentatively, then stopped as she saw the warning look in his eyes.

'Yes?' he enquired with icy calm.

'I was wondering when you're going to present me with a bill for Safiah's treatment. I know you said we should wait until there was some improvement, but you must realise by now that the case is hopeless . . .'

'Safiah can walk,' he put in quietly.

Anna stared at him in stunned silence for a few moments before she could find her voice.

'What did you say?' she asked incredulously.

'I said that Safiah can walk.'

'But I don't understand!' she stammered.

'Neither did I at first. More coffee?' he asked calmly.

She shook her head. 'Go on, please.'

'Basically, it's a psychological problem,' Simon began, leaning back in his chair as he watched her reaction carefully. 'She suffered concussion when the car crashed. When she came round in the hospital her legs were badly bruised and she got a lot of attention. She was distraught when she learned that Ibrahim had died. Her only source of comfort was in the care lavished upon her by the medical staff.'

'So she decided to prolong her illness? Is that what you're trying to tell me?' Anna's voice was raised shrilly as she tried to make sense of what he was telling her.

'The doctor in charge at Kedang has since been dismissed for incompetence. In fact, it was the man we discussed at our dinner party. He was left behind in the jungle after the second world war. He'd been a medical orderly and had picked up a smattering of medical knowledge. No one checked his credentials during those difficult days, just after the war, and he passed himself off as a surgeon, adding to his basic knowledge as he went along.' Simon paused and reached across the table to take her hand in his.

It was their first physical contact since that fateful night, all those weeks ago, and she shuddered as if an electric current had passed through her.

'For years he practised medicine at Kedang and somehow managed to get away with it. But as the hospital grew from a small field station to a large district hospital, he had to become more careful. When he examined your mother-in-law, she told me he had been extremely kind. But although she told him her head was aching, he did nothing about it. So she decided to get more sympathy by complaining about her legs. She said they wouldn't move, and after a brief examination, he declared that she was paralysed . . .'

'I don't believe it!' Anna pulled her hand away. He's only being kind because I'm so upset, she thought angrily.

'It's true. Safiah told me herself during one of our long conversations,' Simon continued.

'I see; so that's what you were talking about, is it?' The pieces of the puzzle were beginning to fit together. 'But how did you know the problem was psychological?'

He smiled. 'I had a stroke of luck. Do you remember the day I called for you and you had already set off with Razali?'

She nodded, her eyes widening in anticipation.

'Safiah had decided the coast was clear and gone into the garden for her morning exercise—oh yes, she knew that if she didn't use her legs, they really would seize up on her.'

'But surely Zaleha must have seen her?' Anna cried in disbelief.

'Zaleha was in on it too, but she's been keeping up the pretence because she was afraid she'd lose her job. Safiah told her the whole story soon after she was first employed, but she told her to keep quiet.'

'It seems a very pathetic way of getting attention,' she said softly.

'She was a very pathetic woman after the accident,' Simon explained. 'The concussion had affected her brain. In the hands of a qualified doctor she would have been thoroughly examined for brain damage. She got used to pretending, and found she could get away with it . . .'

'But why? I would have looked after her, anyway.'

'Would you?' he asked drily. 'She told me you'd quarrelled with Ibrahim on the day of the crash and she'd taken his side, as she always did on these occasions. She was afraid you would hate her for the things she'd said to you . . .'

'Stop it!' she screamed at him. The whole dreadful incident came flooding back. Yes, she had hated Safiah for the way she had been treated, but she would never have held it against her if she had needed help. If Simon knew the whole story he would understand—but she couldn't bring herself to tell him . . .

'She also said you were taken into hospital yourself on the day of the crash, but she wouldn't tell me why.'

His voice was low and sympathetic. This is how he wormed everything out of Safiah, Anna thought warily. But he's not going to get anything out of me. She stood up calmly and walked away from him. At the door to the house, she turned.

'If she wouldn't tell you, then neither will I,' she said firmly. 'I appreciate all you've done for her. If you'll let me have your bill . . .'

'Why are you so antagonistic towards me?' he shouted, crossing the verandah with long easy strides to tower above her.

For a moment she thought he was going to strike her.

'I'm not being antagonistic,' she retorted. 'It just takes time for me to digest what you've been saying. For the past three years, I've believed my mother-in-law to be paralysed. Now you tell me it was all a pretence . . . That takes some getting used to.'

'Of course it does . . . I'm sorry.'

She looked up into his eyes at the sound of his sympathetic voice and her heart turned over. I'm not antagonistic towards you, she wanted to tell him. I daren't give in to my true feelings. It wouldn't be fair. Things have gone too far as it is . . .

'I'm going to arrange for her to see a psychiatrist when she feels up to it,' Simon continued. 'Although I've known she could walk ever since I met her, it was only last week that she broke down and told me the whole story . . .'

'This doctor—the one who examined her,' Anna interrupted quickly. 'What happened to him?'

'He disappeared for a while, but from time to time I've heard about him. I think he's hiding out on the island somewhere,' he replied cautiously.

'Here on Desaman?' she queried anxiously.

'Yes . . . and when I find him, I'll kill him!' was his whispered reply.

A chill ran down her spine as she saw the desperate expression masking the handsome features. She had never seen such a look of pure hatred on anyone's face. They both stood rooted to the spot, until Simon moved suddenly away.

'There's work to be done,' he muttered grimly.

Thank goodness for work! thought Anna, as she followed him inside. For a moment she had expected the doctor to storm off on a lethal mission. He couldn't really hate someone because they were incompetent, could he? Not enough to want to kill them, surely? She shivered, in spite of the intense heat.

The villagers started to drift in to their clinic as soon as the door was opened. It seemed that everyone wanted to have a look inside the newly converted medical house, and the real illnesses were few and far between. There was nothing that couldn't be handled on the island. The medical launch was standing by, just in case it was needed to take a patient back to Penasing.

Anna was pleased that the response to their work was so gratifying. The mothers brought their babies to be weighed and discussed their problems with her and with each other, sitting outside for hours after they had been seen by the doctor.

Kandiah arrived with her baby boy, and he was duly admired by the doctor and nurse who had performed the Caesarian section at his birth. To Anna it seemed like a lifetime ago, although it was only a few weeks. But so much had happened since then.

There was another young mother that she recognised. Simon had managed to persuade her to go over to Penasing for the birth of her baby, and she had avoided complications of high blood pressure.

All in all, it was a very satisfying sort of day, she told herself, as she sat outside on the verandah with a cold drink of mango juice in her hand. She had ne idea where Simon was. He had disappeared at the end of the clinic. Now that she had settled Magdi down for the night, she could have some time to herself.

The dark red sun was low on the horizon, casting a rosy glow over the blue sea. She could see the hospital launch moored by the jetty. So Simon hadn't decided to take off by himself. They were close to Tawa and she had thought that maybe he would want to take a trip across the water to see Coral . . .

Her thoughts were confused as she watched the sun disappear into the sea. She realised that she was delighted that Safiah could walk. It had been such a shock when Simon told her. It was only now that she remembered the occasions when she thought she had detected some movement of the lower limbs as she helped Zaleha to lift Safiah into bed. She had pointed it out once, and begged her mother-in-law to allow a doctor to examine her. But the matriarch had been adamant—no doctors; no hospitals. And Zaleha had agreed with her mistress.

Anna smiled. It was all becoming clear to her at last . . . the whispered conversations between the two women that ceased when she entered the room . . . the blanket over the legs in spite of the tropical temperature. And the fact that Zaleha could put her mother-in-law to bed, unaided, when she found it impossible. She had thought that Zaleha must be endowed with superhuman strength . . .

'What are you smiling about?'

She jumped as she heard Simon's unexpected voice from the shadowy palm trees in front of the medical house.

'I was just thinking how happy I am that Safiah can walk,' she replied quickly.

He stepped out of the shadows and strode across the clearing. As he climbed the steps to the verandah, she thought how strong and muscular he looked in the twilight, like some athletic prince from outer space who had decided to land on the island and would soon vanish again.

'It's going to change my life considerably,' she continued quickly, as he sank down on one of the cane chairs beside her.

'In what way?' he asked, his eyes narrowing shrewdly.

'Well, if she can walk, then she's not going to need me as much.'

'I don't want you to make any changes until she's been seen by a psychiatrist,' he rapped out. 'You must keep up the pretence for the moment.'

'But . . . I'd like to tell Razali,' she faltered.

'Of course,' he replied distantly. 'He seems a very sensible sort of man.'

'I'd like to go down and see him in Singapore this weekend . . . to explain the situation. He has a right to know.'

'I'm sure Sister Kasim will give you a weekend pass.'

'I hope so!' said Anna with a warmth of feeling that he couldn't understand. How could he know what was uppermost in her mind at the moment? She had only come to the momentous decision herself today.

Simon stared at her quizzically. 'Are you feeling all right, Anna?' he asked.

'Perfectly. Never felt better.'

'Good, because I'm afraid I'll have to leave you alone tonight.'

So he's going over to see Coral, she thought miserably.

'. . . There's something I have to do,' he continued earnestly.

'What time will you bring the boat back for me?' she asked in a cool voice. 'I don't want to be left stranded here all day.'

'I'm not taking the boat,' he replied sharply. 'I have to go up into the mountains to look for someone.'

'Ah yes, the mystery *doktor*,' she breathed, as she saw the tense expression on his face. 'Why do you hate him so much?'

'Because he's a menace to the community and . . .' he paused, as if searching for the right words, '. . . and I've got an old score to settle with him. I've waited a long time.'

He stood up and paced the verandah restlessly. Suddenly he stopped as he reached her chair and, leaning down, put his hands on her shoulders so that he could look directly into her eyes.

'Are you sure you'll be all right by yourself?' he asked softly.

Anna's heart thumped madly at the nearness of that virile body. She wanted to put her arms out towards him and tell him that no, she would miss him terribly. But she knew she mustn't . . . especially now . . .

'I'll be fine,' she murmured quickly.

'Lock the door and stay inside until I return.' For a moment his grip on her tightened, but he straightened his back decisively and moved away.

She watched as he strode off towards the

mountain path. As he started to climb up through the jungle trees, she went inside and bolted the door.

CHAPTER NINE

SHE WAS awakened next morning by the sound of loud voices. Looking through the wooden louvred window, she saw that the village was swarming with policemen! Oh no! She rushed into Simon's room, praying that he had come back. But the bed hadn't been slept in. Her mind was in turmoil.

She remembered his veiled threats . . . 'If I find him, I'll kill him,' he had said. 'I've got an old score to settle . . .'

But he's a doctor, Anna told herself comfortingly. He's sworn to save life, not to take it away. But how well did she know him? Could she be sure that in an irrational moment he might . . .

Pulling on her white cotton dress, she went outside into the early morning sunlight. The police contingent had moved through the village and were climbing back into their jeep on the outskirts. Down by the jetty she could see the ferry boat that had transported them here from the mainland. She watched as the jeep revved up to take a run at the rough mountain track. A Malay villager was returning from giving them directions, and Anna recognised her friend Mohammed, Kandiah's husband.

'What do they want?' she asked quickly, running down the path to meet him.

'They are looking for Dr Sinclair,' he replied gravely.

Her heart went cold. There wasn't a second to lose. She had to get there first. Whatever he had done, she loved Simon. She always would, and even though they could never be together, she didn't want him to come to any harm.

'Is there a quicker way up the mountain, Mohammed?' she demanded breathlessly.

He looked surprised. 'There is the path through the jungle, but it is very steep . . .'

'Show me the way—please!' she pleaded desperately.

'Follow me.' He turned and retraced his steps.

As they reached the outskirts of the village, he cut up through the trees. Anna went after him, grasping at branches with which to haul herself up the steeper sections. Her dress tore on a prickly plant, her hands were scratched by the rough branches, but her only thought was that she must get there in time.

At last the path emerged from the jungle on to a narrow track.

'This is the track from the village,' Mohammed explained. 'You are ahead of the policemen. They will pass this way soon . . .'

'Thank you, Mohammed,' she said quickly. 'I'll go alone from here.'

'*Selamat tinggal.*' The young Malay disappeared back into the jungle, anxious to return to his family.

Anna looked up at the mountain track. Monsoon rains had carved deep scars over its surface. It would be difficult, if not impossible, to negotiate it in a jeep . . . and she was ahead of them . . .

She climbed higher up the track. Supposing Simon wasn't up here . . . supposing she had

missed him altogether . . . ? And then she saw a
rough path leading off to the right. A tiny scrap of
white cotton was clinging to a bush.

He was wearing a white shirt, she told herself
excitedly. This must be the way.

Several yards along the path she stopped to catch
her breath. There in a small clearing was a tiny
wooden hut, its roof thatched with reeds and palm
leaves. Sitting in the open doorway was Simon, his
dark hair hanging over his forehead.

'You're too late,' he said quietly. 'He's dead.'

'Simon, you fool!' Anna flung herself at him, but
he restrained her.

'No, don't go in there!'

Through the open doorway she had caught a
glimpse of a squalid room and in the centre a rough
blanket had been thrown over a body. Simon held
her against him, and she found comfort in his
strength.

'Why do you say I'm a fool . . . and what are you
doing up here?' His arms tightened their grip and
she relaxed against him, wanting to shut out the
real world. There was so little time for them to be
together.

'I wanted to get here before you . . . to stop
you . . .' Tears were running down her cheeks as
her voice choked. It was impossible to go on.

'My poor little Anna,' he whispered soothingly.
'You don't think I had anything to do with his
death, do you?'

'But you said . . .' she faltered.

'People say a lot of things, in the heat of the
moment, that they don't mean. My main concern
was to stop the man making any more medical
blunders.'

'But what about the old score you had to settle?' she pursued relentlessly.

'Ah, that's a long story . . .'

There was the sound of voices coming up the path.

'That's the police,' Anna told him anxiously.

'I know,' he said. 'I sent for them last night. They agreed to come at first light. I thought we might have a struggle on our hands, but in the event, he was dying when I arrived.'

'He was dying—so you witnessed his death?'

'Yes.' He seemed weary of her questions as he stood up to greet the men emerging through the trees. 'Good morning, Captain.'

Anna's mind was in a whirl as she watched the uniformed men going into the little hut. Simon was explaining about the death, writing things down in a large book. The Captain was asking endless questions, but in the end he seemed satisfied. The men removed the body, carrying it down to where they had been forced to abandon their jeep. They were offered a lift, but Anna gave a shake of her head and Simon sensed that she would prefer to walk back.

As the last man disappeared through the trees, she turned to Simon again.

'But who was he?' she asked, wanting to solve the riddle once and for all.

He took a deep breath before answering. 'He called himself Doktor Smith. The Malays thought he was English, and the English thought he was of mixed race. He spoke several languages fluently, so no one was ever sure where he came from. Just before he died he told me about his early life. I think then I came to understand—if not orgive—what he did.'

His voice trembled with emotion and he paused or a few moments.

'Go on,' Anna whispered encouragingly.

'He was born in Calcutta to an Indian prostitute. His father was unknown to him, but his mother laimed he was an English sailor. He spent his hildhood begging on the streets of Calcutta. He oined up at the beginning of the war and finished p in Malaya, fighting in the jungle. He became eparated from his unit and had to survive on his wn. When the war ended, he passed himself off as doctor at the medical field station of Kedang. 'hey were only too grateful for his help, and didn't heck up on him. But he was always afraid he might e found out, and he started to drink heavily . . .'

'Was this when he gave himself away?' she asked uietly.

'This was when he started to make mistakes,' imon replied, his blue eyes flashing. 'This was the ause of his downfall, in more ways than one. When arrived here last night I found him in the last tages of cirrhosis of the liver. I won't give you the etails,' he added hurriedly. 'I only hope you never ave to witness anything like it.'

She shuddered. 'Were you able to help him?'

He gave a weak smile. 'He had no idea who I vas, but he begged me to give him a drink. I knew e couldn't last the night, so I gave him the last regs from his bottle. There was nothing more I ould do, except stay with him through the night. ronic, isn't it, that the alcohol that poisoned him vas his comfort as he died. What a waste of a life!'

'You said he didn't know you; but I thought you ad some kind of vendetta?'

'You ask too many questions.' He stood up and pulled her to her feet. 'This place depresses me; let's go.'

Anna scrambled down the jungle path behind him. A family of monkeys was swinging easily through the trees, chattering noisily to each other as they watched the intruders from a safe distance. Simon turned, only once, to help her when she stumbled and fell. He put his arms round her waist and lifted her back on her feet.

She was standing on higher ground and their eyes were level. For one heart-stopping moment she thought he was going to kiss her. There was a tender look in his eyes.

'Are you OK?' he asked, in a concerned voice.

She nodded. 'I'll survive.' She was desperately tired, longing for a bath.

When they reached the village she made straight for her room and tore off the filthy dress. This time she had come prepared; there had been a bikini in her travel bag ever since her first visit to Desaman. She was not going to get caught out again!

The water in the stream was like soothing lotion to her hot skin. She revelled in its clear depth before lying on her back amid the palm frond between two large rocks.

'We'll have to go, Anna.' Simon had come to find where she was and was looking irritated, as he stood on the bank.

'What's the rush? I thought we were going to leave this evening.' Anna pulled herself to a sitting position, noticing that he was fully dressed in immaculate slacks and shirt.

'I have to make a call on Tawa,' he replied hurriedly.

So that was it! She stood up and reached for her towel. 'I'll be ready in a few minutes,' she said shortly. 'But I want to check on Magdi first.'

'I've just been there. The girl is coping very well. There's nothing you need do.'

'Even so, I'd like to see for myself.'

He went with her to Magdi's house when she was dressed, and together they said goodbye to their little patient and his young nurse. As they went down to the waiting boat Anna felt sad. She didn't know when she would see Desaman again.

A strong monsoon wind was springing up as they went across the water towards Tawa. Neither of them spoke until they reached the jetty. Coral was waiting on the beach, and she waved excitedly as the boat pulled in, running along to meet Simon on her bare, sandy feet.

'No need to tie up,' Simon told the skipper, as he leapt ashore. 'Goodbye, Anna.'

'Goodbye,' she replied firmly.

Huge drops of rain began to pelt the surface of the sea as they headed for Penasing. Big black clouds obscured the sun and the wind whipped white foam on to the tops of the waves. This time it really is goodbye, she thought. There's no going back now.

A huge crowd had gathered on the quayside as they pulled in to Penasing. Amid the confusion she could hear the sound of an ambulance siren. Immediately on the alert, she noticed signs of wreckage in the water.

'Hurry, there's some emergency!' she shouted to the skipper.

Through the driving rain she could make out the

shape of the Penasing lifeboat, only yards away from them.

'What's the trouble?' she called.

'There's a car in the water,' came the chilling reply. 'We're trying to locate the occupants.'

Anna jumped ashore as soon as they were tied up. 'What happened?' she asked one of the spectators.

'A taxi was reversing and he skidded on the wet surface and plunged into the sea. There are six of them down there.'

'Oh, no!' Even as she spoke, she saw one of the lifeboatmen plunging down into the murky depths.

The crowd waited, unusually quiet. As he emerged minutes later with a child held firmly in his grasp, the crowd cheered. 'We've got the door open!' he called breathlessly.

Two bedraggled men appeared, their arms flailing desperately at the surface of the water, as the lifeboatmen pulled them to safety.

Several of the crowd had dived in to help with the rescue operation. Anna hurried along to the ambulance. As the child was brought in she felt for his pulse. There was a faint sign that the heart was still beating, but the boy's face was congested and livid in colour. She turned him on his side to evacuate the foam-like froth that was obstructing the passage of air to his lungs. When she was sure this was clear, she began resuscitation.

Opening her mouth wide, she took a deep breath, before sealing her lips around his mouth and nose. Then she gently blew into his lungs. After several anxious seconds the little chest started to rise. Anna removed her mouth and waited for the chest to fall. She repeated the process as rapidly as possible in an attempt to saturate the blood with oxygen. After the first four successful inflations, she reduced the pace until she saw that her patient was breathing naturally.

Exhausted, she leaned back against the side of the ambulance and stared in surprise at the blue eyes gazing down on her.

'Simon?' she muttered, as she tried to get her breath back.

'I didn't mean to startle you. I got an emergency call to come and help. You handled that very well.'

'Thanks,' she said shortly. 'How are the others?'

'They're all up. I've got three in the next ambulance—all breathing, thank goodness. Will you take these two in here?'

'Of course.' She wrapped blankets round the two bedraggled men. In spite of the heat, they were shivering violently.

'See you back at the hospital,' Simon said quickly as he closed up the doors.

As she returned to her little patient, Anna thought she had never intended it to work out like this. Every time she planned to escape, fate seemed to take a hand. But she would have to speak to Simon when the emergency was over.

They worked together side by side in Casualty, all through the rest of the day. Miraculously, the six patients survived and didn't suffer any lasting damage to their lungs. They were all admitted, but Simon said he didn't foresee any complications.

As they cleared up the debris he suddenly turned to Anna and put his hand on her arm.

'Come and have supper with me,' he said. 'Leave this for the night staff. You've worked hard enough tonight.'

'There's something I have to tell you . . .' she began, but he interrupted her.

'Tell me later . . . over supper.' He was grinning boyishly.

She hadn't seen him like this for weeks. 'I really should get back to Safiah . . .' she began.

'Nonsense. She can put herself to bed—Zaleha will help. It's almost as if you have a guilt complex about the woman!'

'Don't say that,' she snapped. If he only knew! 'I'd like to have supper with you,' she added quickly in a gentler tone.

Perhaps this would be a good time to sort things out, she thought, as she went to the locker room to change into mufti. At least she wouldn't have to accept charity in the shape of a borrowed dress this evening! She had made sure that Coral's dress was returned in pristine condition. It had been a fabulous dress, but she didn't want to repeat the experience.

She had assumed, quite rightly, that Simon would take her to the Sinclair residence. What she hadn't bargained for was that they would be alone except for a couple of discreet servants who hovered in the background as they sat on the verandah. Wherever Sir Lawrence had gone, he had taken most of his staff with him.

One of the stewards placed an ice bucket with a bottle of champagne beside Simon.

'What are we celebrating?' asked Anna, as they raised their glasses.

'Do we need a reason?' he asked solemnly.

She noticed that his eyes were smiling. He looked happier than she had seen him for a long time. She took a tentative sip and their eyes met above their glasses.

'You're right—there is a reason.' His voice was husky. He put down his glass on a low table and stared out towards the sea.

The monsoon winds had disappeared as quickly as they arrived. The clouds had vanished and there was nothing to obscure the pale light of the moon.

'I said I had a score to settle with Dr Smith,' he began, without looking at her. 'It all happened a long time ago . . .'

Anna shivered at the ominous tone of his voice.

'When I was a young medical student I fell in love with Stephanie. She was a nurse at St Celine's in London, where I trained. We were very much in love . . .' His voice cracked with emotion.

Anna had never seen him like this. She had known his passion, but never such deep emotion.

'How old were you?' she asked gently.

'We were twenty-one when we married,' he answered nostalgically. 'Steph had just got her SRN. I had another three years before I qualified, but we didn't want to wait. We wanted to start a family immediately—and we did!' He smiled and some of the tension was reduced.

'My father was over the moon when I told him Steph was pregnant. The only problem was that the expected date of confinement coincided with my exams. Dad suggested we both come out during my vacation and Steph could stay on to be cared for here. He engaged a local midwife, and the servants also took great care of her.'

He paused, and Anna knew from his tone that something dreadful had happened.

'Don't go on if it upsets you,' she offered gently.

'I'm OK . . . When I left her here, to go back to

London, I was perfectly satisfied with the arrangements. She was young, in perfect health. No one could have foreseen any problems. Two weeks before the birth, the baby turned into a breech position. The midwife noticed this and insisted that they go to Kedang hospital. The doctor on duty admitted Steph and said there was no need to worry, he would take care of her himself. That doctor was Dr Smith . . .'

Anna took a deep breath, anticipating the worst.

'I don't know how long she was in labour before she died,' Simon continued. 'But I vowed then and there that I'd have the charlatan strung up if I ever got my hands on him . . . My father dissuaded me from pursuing the matter at that time. Stephanie was dead; nothing would bring her back. A Caesarian would have saved her, but I knew that Dr Smith had argued against this. At the time, I had no idea just how limited his medical knowledge was.'

'You must have been heartbroken,' Anna said softly.

'I was.' He reached for her hand, holding it gently in his own, as if in need of her comfort. 'But I was young and I had my medical career to think about. I got on with my studies, but I promised myself I'd see the man brought to justice, and until I did, I wouldn't allow myself to fall in love . . . After I qualified, I was too busy to do anything about him. Then I was asked to come out here to start up the surgical unit and the islands project. I kept hearing stories of Dr Smith's incompetence. By this time he'd been dismissed for drinking too much. Only after he disappeared was it discovered

hat his incompetence amounted to criminal
negligence.'

'And you found him on Desaman,' she breathed.

'Yes, I found him—an old, harmless man. All
my desire for revenge vanished when I saw the
pathetic creature. I made him comfortable, gave
him a drink and waited for the end . . . You know
the rest.'

'I'm glad you told me,' she said quietly.

'So am I. Now you understand what a relief it is
for me to have wiped the slate clean. I can start all
over again. I can fall in love and get married . . .'

Oh yes, Anna understood perfectly! She remembered Daphne Squires' words: It's only a question
of time before he realises he's in love with her. Was
that why he had called in at Tawa? To tell Coral
that he was free at last? He had exorcised his
revenge?

Dinner is served, sir.' A white-coated steward was
standing by Simon's chair.

'Thank you, Musa. Shall we go in?' He was
smiling happily, as if a great load had been lifted
from his shoulders.

They sat together at one end of the long polished
table. Simon was in high spirits, as if he hadn't a
care in the world. Anna tried to enter into the
carefree mood, but her heart was heavy. It was not
a good time to tender her resignation, but it had to
be done. She waited until they had reached the
coffee stage. It's best not to spoil this delicious
meal, she thought.

It was obvious that the two young Malay stewards had gone to a lot of trouble preparing the
meal. She wondered if they were surprised—or

even shocked—at her appearance that evening.
Maybe the meal had been specially prepared
for Coral. It had certainly been a lavish affair;
several courses starting with a magnificent lobster
and finishing with a coffee mousse, whipped to
perfection.

Simon had been too polite to remark on her lack
of appetite, but she had found the meal a strain.
She wanted to say what had to be said and leave
him, as quickly as possible. A clean break was the
only way.

She put down her tiny china coffee cup.

'Simon . . .' she began tentatively.

'You're wanted on the telephone, sir. It's the
hospital. They say it's urgent,' announced Musa in
a deferential voice.

The surgeon crossed the room in easy strides and
disappeared into the hall. Anna waited with bated
breath. Was it one of the newly-admitted patients?

He returned, his carefree manner replaced by
cool professionalism.

'It's Talik—the driver of the taxi. Sister Kasim
says he's complaining of increased pain in the chest
and difficulty in breathing. Will you come with
me?' he asked abruptly.

'Of course.' She was instantly on her feet, knowing she had no choice. Her car was down at the
hospital and she didn't want to wait around here
until he returned. Besides, she was worried about
Talik; it sounded like a pneumothorax.

Sister Kasim showed no surprise when they
arrived together at the hospital.

'I'm glad you came too, Staff Nurse,' she said
with a brief smile. 'You admitted this patient
didn't you? I'm helping Dr Singh with a difficul

ase in Obstetrics. Would you mind assisting Dr
inclair?'

'Not at all, Sister. I'd like to see this thing
hrough.'

They were hurrying down the corridor towards
Vad Laki—the men's ward.

Simon took one look at Talik and whispered,
Pneumothorax. Get me a Morland's chest needle
nd a small-size trocar and canular. Do we have an
rtificial pneumothorax machine?'

Anna nodded. 'I'll get it here.'

Simon glanced at the X-rays. 'This rib fracture
nust have punctured the lung. I'll have to remove
he air from the pleural space . . .'

She held Talik's hand as the life-saving needle
vas inserted. As Simon connected it to the machine
he dangerous air pressure was reduced and the
vatient began to breathe more easily.

'That's better,' Anna said softly.

'Thanks for your help.' Their eyes met across the
vatient.

She turned her attention on Talik. There was a
ump in her throat. This was definitely the last time
he would assist Simon . . .

'I can take over now.' Sister Kasim bustled
vack into Wad Laki. 'My patient in Obstetrics
las a healthy baby boy, and the night staff are
coping admirably. You'd better run along,
Vurse Gabell, or you won't be fit for duty in the
norning.'

'Sister, I wonder if I might have a weekend pass.
have to go down to Singapore to see my brother-
n-law . . . on a personal matter,' Anna added
lurriedly.

'Is it urgent?' asked Sister.

'Yes, it is,' she replied, aware that Simon was watching her.

'In that case you must go, of course. We have some extra staff at the moment, so I can replace you. I take it you have no objection, Dr Sinclair. You won't be needing Staff Nurse this weekend?' asked the older woman.

'No, I won't be needing her,' he replied coldly. He bent over the patient to adjust the needle.

Anna moved towards the door. 'Good night,' she said softly.

'Good night,' returned Sister Kasim.

But there was no reply from the surgeon.

CHAPTER TEN

ANNA STARED out of the window of the Singapore
nursing home. Had she really been here only two
days? It seemed like a lifetime since she had arrived
here with Fay. What a good friend the Theatre
Sister had proved to be, when she had told her of
her dilemma.

Above the harbour she could see a cable car
suspended above the water, on its way to the island
of Sentosa. Razali had taken her there on Sunday.
He had been delighted to see her when she arrived
at his flat, unexpectedly, on Saturday. There had
been so much to talk about. He was overjoyed to
hear that his mother could walk, but it wasn't until
they spent a long, lazy day on Sentosa that he told
her his own wonderful news. He was going to be
married!

He had met up with an old school friend, who
was working as a secretary in Singapore. His own
career was flourishing. And they were both so
much in love.

'We see no reason to wait,' he had told Anna
breathlessly. 'We're both twenty-nine . . .'

'Positively over the hill!' she had quipped. 'I'm
absolutely delighted for you. So when's the
wedding?'

'As soon as it can be arranged. I was worried
about Mother, but now it will be easier. I wonder—' he paused, choosing his words carefully,
'do you think you could ask your colleague, Dr

Sinclair, if he could arrange Mother's psychiatri‹
treatment in Singapore? You see, it would be s‹
nice if she could come and live with us here. I thin‹
she'd like that, don't you?'

'I'm sure she'd be delighted.' Anna's brain ha‹
been working overtime. 'I'll send a message to D‹
Sinclair.'

'I thought you would be seeing him tomorrow,
he said, giving her a puzzled look.

'I have some medical business to see to here i‹
Singapore, so I shan't be going back—for a while,
she added, to stop any further questions. 'What d‹
you think we should do about Zaleha?'

'She's not such a bad sort, really,' Razali repli‹
thoughtfully. 'She's very loyal to Mother—to‹
loyal!'

Anna laughed. 'Can you afford to keep her on a‹
Mother's maid?'

'Sure. We shall both be earning, initially, an‹
then when the babies come along, she'll be invalu‹
able.' He looked excited at the prospect of settin‹
up his own home.

'Well, that's settled, then,' Anna said, with ‹
note of finality.

He looked at her anxiously. 'I hope you won't b‹
lonely by youself, Anna? I mean, you've got you‹
career, haven't you? And you'll be very welcome i‹
my house, whenever you want to come.'

'You've been very kind, Razali. I don't kno‹
what I would have done without you,' she had tol‹
him gratefully.

He had driven her to the National Universit‹
Hospital in his new car. Mercifully, he hadn't aske‹
her any more questions.

She had found her own way to Theatre an‹

ught Fay just as she was going off duty. It didn't
ke Fay long to understand the problem, and
fore nightfall, Anna had been booked in at the
angri-La Nursing Home, overlooking the busy
rbour. That was two days ago, two days in which
e had experienced every emotion but despair.
e was still hopeful . . .

The door to her private room opened and her
nsultant stood there, smiling at her reassuringly.
e crossed the thick pile carpet and sat down on
r bed.

'I have the results of your tests. There's only one
oblem . . .' He stopped in mid-sentence as the
or opened again.

Simon stood framed in the doorway, his face as
ack as thunder.

'What are you doing here?' gasped Anna.

'I was going to ask you the same question,' he
apped, then remembering his professional eti-
uette, he held out his hand to the consultant. 'I'm
mon Sinclair. I hope you don't mind me barging
like this.'

'That's quite all right, Dr Sinclair. I remember
u from a conference in London last year. I'm
arry Burnett.'

The two men exchanged polite conversation for a
w moments, leaving Anna to lie back on her
llows staring up at the ceiling.

'I'll come back later when Dr Sinclair has gone,'
id the young consultant. 'We shall need time to
scuss what we're going to do.'

'Please don't go . . .' she began quickly, but
mon interrupted her.

'I think it would be a good idea if we had a
nversation in private, Anna. You've got some

explaining to do.'

The other man took the hint and left them on their own. As the door closed, she turned to face him, her eyes blazing with anger.

'You've no right to come here, throwing your weight around! I'm a private patient here. And you have no control over me. I've already sent my resignation to Penasing . . .'

'I know; that's why I'm here,' he told her.

'But how on earth did you find me? No one knew where I was—except Fay . . .' Her voice trailed away.

'Exactly. When I got your resignation, I thought you must have stayed on in Singapore with Razali. I rang him, but he said he'd dropped you at the University Hospital and you had some medical business to attend to. So I rang Fay . . .'

'Quite the detective, aren't you!' Anna flung at him.

'At first she wouldn't tell me where you were . . .'

'And then you wormed it out of her like you always do.' She was crying with frustration. She had tried so hard to escape him.

'She said it was probably the best thing if I came to see you. So I left everything and came at once.'

'But why? Why can't you leave me alone?' she screamed through her tears.

'Because I love you, Anna. And I'm not going to let you go,' Simon whispered softly, as he sat down on the bed and took her in his arms.

She stiffened at his touch. It couldn't possibly be true! She'd heard him wrong . . . he didn't love her. He was in love with Coral . . .

'What did you say?' she sobbed as she tried to pull away from those strong arms.

'I said I love you,' he repeated firmly. 'I wanted to tell you the other night. I was leading up to it when I told you I was free to marry. And then we were called to the hospital . . .'

'But what about Coral?' she asked, unable to take in his words.

'What about her?' He looked puzzled.

'I thought you were in love with her . . .'

He was laughing now, cradling her against him like a baby. She could feel his strong rib-cage and her resolve began to weaken. It was impossible to fight a man like this.

'I don't know whatever gave you that idea. Coral is going to marry my father. He's finally popped the question—and not before time! The poor girl had practically given up hope. She started as his secretary—years ago. And it was love at first sight for her, but he's taken more persuasion. She just kept on making herself more and more indispensable until finally he realised he was in love with her.' He paused as he saw the light dawning on her.

'That's what Daphne said would happen, but I thought she was talking about you . . .'

'About me?' he echoed. 'I can't think how you could possibly have been misled. I'm terribly fond of Coral. She's like a sister to me, and she runs the house beautifully,' he grinned.

'So therefore she's got to stay with the family. I suppose you've got used to working with me and you don't want to lose a good nurse . . .'

'It's got nothing to do with whether or not you're a good nurse. I'm asking you to be my wife.'

'Don't say it, Simon,' she cried out. 'I told Fay she wasn't to tell you. You're only taking pity on me . . .'

'What on earth are you talking about?' he asked in a low, husky voice.

'You mean Fay didn't tell you?'

'Tell me what?'

She took a deep breath. Either he was a very good actor or he really didn't know.

'I'm pregnant,' she told him quietly.

He stared at her in stunned disbelief.

'So Fay didn't tell you,' Anna whispered as she watched his reaction.

'She most certainly did not. I hadn't the slightest idea.'

'I thought you were asking me to marry you because it was your duty . . .' she began, but his arms tightened around her

'You mean it's mine?' Simon's voice cracked with emotion.

'Of course it's yours. I hope you don't think I go around making love indiscriminately. It was that night on Tawa. I shouldn't have given in to my feelings like I did. There's been no one since my husband died . . .'

'Oh, my darling, I'm so glad you let me make love to you. I wanted to tell you how much I loved you. But I was hell-bent on finishing my vendetta . . . I was so near to revenge that I didn't want anything to stop me. And now it's all over and I'm free to marry . . .'

'But you don't understand,' she broke in desperately. 'There are complications . . .'

'What sort of complications?' he asked impatiently.

'Medical.'

'We'll sort it out,' he persisted. 'Anna, do you love me?'

'Yes—oh yes, I love you.'

He took her face in his strong surgeon's hands and covered it with kisses.

As he pulled away, he murmured, 'That's all I need to know. Marry me, Anna. Whatever the problem is, we can face it together.'

'No! I can't condemn you to a childless marriage!' Her voice rang out painfully in the little room.

For a moment he stared at her in stunned silence. 'But you told me you were pregnant,' he whispered.

She looked up into the face of the man she loved so much. A puzzled frown had creased his aristocratic brow and a nerve was twitching in his cheek. I care about him too much to let him marry me, she thought, checking all her natural instincts. I've got to let him go.

A choking sob rose in her throat as she watched the tender expression in his blue eyes.

'I can't go through with the pregnancy,' she began in a faltering voice. 'After my miscarriage, three years ago, I was told I must never get pregnant again. In fact, I was advised to have a sterilisation . . . But I couldn't bear any more pain and suffering, at the time.'

Simon held her closer in his arms and she leaned against him. For this one last time she would allow herself to be near him . . . to pretend that it would last . . .

'You told me it was around the time of your husband's death,' he prompted her gently, stroking back the dark hair that had fallen over her damp forehead.

'It was the longest day of my life,' she murmured, almost to herself. She stared into the gentle eyes and suddenly she wanted to unburden herself. She had never told anyone what had really happened on that dreadful day. It had been bottled up inside her for too long.

'I feel so guilty.' She took a deep breath, and forced herself to continue. 'I was going to leave Ibrahim. My mother had sent me some money —not much, but it was enough to buy an air ticket back to the UK. I'd had enough. When I told Ibrahim, on that last morning, he was furious. He told me it was my duty to stay. He threatened me . . . and then he became violent. His mother heard the noise and came into our room. She told me I was an undutiful daughter-in-law . . . that Ibrahim was quite right to hit me.'

'Did she know you were pregnant?' demanded Simon.

'No, she didn't—I'd told no one . . . not even Ibrahim. You see, I'd been planning to leave him . . . That's why I feel so guilty. If he'd known I was carrying his child, he wouldn't have been so cruel.'

'There's no excuse for cruelty,' Simon rapped out harshly. 'What did he do to you?'

'He sent his mother out to the car and told her to wait for him. Then he raped me . . .' Her voice trailed away; she couldn't continue as the dreadful events flooded back to her.

'He raped you?' Simon repeated in disbelief.

She nodded. 'But I was his wife, and I felt so guilty about hating him. He locked me in our room . . . When the police came to tell me about the crash, they had to break the door down.'

'But you mustn't feel guilty!' he put in angrily. 'He was the one who . . .'

'He was my husband, and it might have been my fault that he crashed the car . . . because he was so angry with me . . .'

'Oh no, it wasn't! I heard a vivid description of the crash from Safiah. It had nothing to do with the way Ibrahim was driving. It was the weather conditions, the monsoon rains—call it an act of God if you like, but don't blame yourself!' Simon pleaded anxiously.

Suddenly Anna began to see things in perspective, for the first time since that fateful day.

'After he had gone,' she continued, 'I started to haemorrhage—but there was nothing I could do . . . until the police found me, and took me to hospital.'

'To Kedang hospital?' he prompted.

She nodded.

'And after the miscarriage, who was it who told you that you should be sterilised?' he asked quickly.

'Why, the doctor in charge, of course. Why do you want to know?'

'Call it professional interest,' he replied quietly. 'Do you remember his name?'

'I was too ill to care about anything,' she answered abruptly. 'Really, Simon, do you have to interrogate me like this? I've told you . . .'

'Was he, by any chance, very tall with a scar on his left cheek?' he pursued relentlessly.

Anna sighed and closed her eyes, trying desperately to remember. And then, through the long-forgotten mists of consciousness, she could see a face peering down at her—a very tall man . . . and yes, he had a scar, because she remembered wondering if he had been a soldier before he took up medicine.

'Yes, that's what he looked like. Do you know him?'

'It was Dr Smith,' Simon told her. 'So you can put aside anything he told you. It's more than likely that your miscarriage was induced by the rough treatment you'd suffered from your husband. But you're in the best place to find out—Harry Burnett is one of Singapore's finest gynaecologists. Has he given you a full examination?'

She nodded. 'But I haven't heard the result of all the tests yet. That's what he was here to tell me. Shall we call him back?'

'Not just yet . . . I want to have you to myself for a while.' He pulled her closer to him and kissed her tenderly on the lips.

Her response was electric. All the pent-up longing of the past weeks was released as she melted against him. The feel of his sensual mouth on hers sent shivers of ecstasy down her spine.

'Oh, Simon, I will marry you if . . .'

'No ifs, my darling,' he said softly, running his fingers through her long hair. 'We belong together whatever happens . . .'

There was a discreet cough as the consultant opened the door. 'I did knock, but you didn't hear me,' began Harry Burnett, his eyes twinkling as he pretended not to have seen their embrace.

'Come in,' Simon invited. 'What have you found?'

The consultant sat down on a chair beside the

bed and placed the tips of his fingers together, as he chose his words carefully.

'We have found that you're in excellent health and you have a perfectly normal, healthy foetus . . .'

'But just now, before Simon arrived, you started to say there was a problem,' Anna put in hurriedly.

He cleared his throat and glanced from one to the other. 'As you may remember, when you came in we discussed the possibility of a termination . . .'

'Never!' thundered Simon. 'This is my child you're talking about!'

'I was going to say that we would be unwilling to perform a termination on a healthy foetus . . .'

'I should hope so too! Darling, what were you thinking about?'

'When I came in, I was expecting to be told of some abnormality. But now . . . Oh, Simon, isn't it wonderful!'

They heard the discreet cough again, and he released her from his arms. Simon gave a wide smile as he leaned across to shake the consultant by the hand.

'Thanks for everything. Is there any reason why I can't take my wife home now?'

'None whatsoever.' Harry Burnett didn't bat an eyelid at the word 'wife'. He was glad he hadn't asked questions about marital status when Anna first arrived. There had obviously been some rift which was now well and truly healed. He thought to himself that he had never seen such happy prospective parents.

She was ready to leave within minutes of hearing the good news. As she stepped into Simon's blue limousine, she felt as if she would burst with happiness.

'Comfortable, Mrs Sinclair?' he asked her with a broad smile.

'You shouldn't call me that . . . yet,' she chided gently.

'I'll soon rectify the problem,' he returned, letting the car cruise quietly down the nursing home drive. 'We'll get a special licence and be married here in Singapore before we go back. And I think we should have a few days' honeymoon while we're here . . . how about Raffles Hotel? Would you like that?'

'But what about your work?'

'Don't be so practical, woman! I asked you if you'd like to go to Raffles for your honeymoon?'

'I'd love it—you know I would . . .'

'OK, Raffles it is—only this time we'll have a whole suite to ourselves.' Simon removed a hand from the wheel to take hers in his own. She gave a contented sigh, and snuggled against him.

'Now, about work . . . I'll ring Ralph and ask him to send one of his bright young doctors and a competent Sister up to Penasing to replace us for a while . . .'

'Talking of Ralph, I must ring Fay at the hospital, to tell her the good news,' Anna broke in quickly.

'Let's go and see them together,' he smiled, as he headed the car towards the National University Hospital. 'And we can invite them to our wedding—it will have to be a quiet affair, but I think we need a couple of guests, don't you?'

She nodded happily. 'And perhaps we should invite Razali and his fiancée.'

CHAPTER ELEVEN

'HEY WERE sitting out on their balcony at Raffles, watching the sun set behind the travellers' palms. Ralph, Fay, Razali and his fiancée had just left hem, sensing that the newlyweds were dying to be lone.

'It's been a wonderful day, Simon,' Anna said blissfully. 'Everything was just perfect.'

'And you didn't mind having a quiet wedding?' e asked gently.

'Who needs people?' she murmured, leaning gainst her husband. 'We were the only ones who eeded to be there.'

'And Razali,' he smiled.

'And Razali,' she agreed with a laugh, re-nembering his surprise when they had asked him nd his girl-friend to act as witnesses to the small ivil ceremony.

'I've fixed up a psychiatrist for Safiah, here in ingapore,' Simon told her.

'You work quickly, don't you?' she said.

He tightened his arms around her. 'Yes, I do. I'm n impatient man—always jumping the gun! But ou'll bear with me, won't you?'

'I'll think about it, doctor.' She reached up and rushed her lips across his. 'But there is one thing 'd like you to explain, before we go to bed. Why lid you have to call in at Tawa, when we were eturning from Desaman? I was terribly jealous!'

He laughed. 'You needn't have been. I was going

to congratulate my father on his engagement to
Coral. He was having a party and everyone was
there—including nearly all the staff.'

'So that's why the house was practically empty
that night,' she murmured.

'I also wanted to tell him the news that I'd
tracked down the bogus doctor and the vendetta
was over. He was glad I'd got that out of my system.
He'd always wanted me to forget it—but you know
what I'm like . . . once I get the bit between my
teeth, nothing will stop me . . .'

'I know,' laughed Anna.

'He told me it was about time I buried the past
and got on with the present. And he said wasn't it
time to admit that I was in love with that fabulous
young nurse . . .'

'Did he say that?' she interrupted him, her eyes
widening.

'Well, not in so many words . . .' he began, but
she had picked up a chintz cushion and aimed it at
his head.

'Simon Sinclair! I don't believe a word of it,' she
cried, shaking with laughter.

'*Mrs* Sinclair, remember your delicate condition!' He scooped her in his arms. 'Time for bed.'

He carried her along the balcony and in through
the long windows of their luxury suite. Gently he
laid her down on the silken sheets of the enormous
bed.

'If you must know, he told me to get the servants
to cook a superb dinner, open a bottle of his best
champagne and seduce you . . .'

'You're wicked!'

'I know,' he agreed, kissing her gently. 'But it
didn't turn out as I expected that night. I was

actually on my way over to Penasing, when I got the
radio message about the submerged car. We coped
with that emergency well enough, but when we
were called out, just as I was about to pop the
question, it was infuriating! Then you asked Sister
Kasim for a weekend pass so that you could go to
see Razali on a personal matter.'

'You didn't think . . . ?'

'Yes, I did! I thought you were in love with him
and I was desperately jealous. But you'd been so
cold and antagonistic towards me . . .'

'*I* was cold! What about you?' laughed Anna.

'Don't let's talk about it any more. It's time you
were in bed, my love. And we shouldn't let our son
stay up late either,' Simon added, with a wide grin.

'Oh, so it's a son, is it?'

'Bound to be,' he answered confidently.

'They didn't do a sex test on me at the nursing
home, did they?' she asked, thinking that maybe
Simon knew something she didn't.

'No, they didn't. Would you like one?'

'No, let's keep it as a surprise.'

CHAPTER TWELVE

HARRY BURNETT straightened up and looked across his patient at the proud new father.

'You were right—it's a boy!'

Simon smiled as he wrapped a cotton blanket around his son, who was announcing his arrival into the world with loud, lusty cries.

'Would you like to hold him, darling?' he asked the new mother.

Anna smiled happily at the sight of her husband and son as she reached out her arms. It had been an easy birth. Harry Burnett had flown up to Penasing, at Simon's request, to be present, but there had been absolutely no complications. In fact, she never remembered a birth that had gone so well—and this time she had been the main character!

'Just like shelling peas!' said Simon, admiration shining in his eyes as he looked down at his wife.

'She's a natural,' the consultant agreed.

'This will be the first of many,' the proud father continued enthusiastically.

'Hey, wait a minute!' Anna put in. 'Do you think I might be consulted first?'

The two doctors laughed.

'I'll need your co-operation, my love, so we'll discuss it later.'

'Much later,' she said firmly. 'Simon needs feeding or he'll wear out his poor little vocal cords.'

Gently she held the infant's little rosebud mouth to her breast and he began to suck.

'Another Simon?' queried the obstetrician.

'It was Anna's choice,' her husband explained, with a wry grin. 'I would have thought one was enough for her.' He sat down on the bed to watch Simon junior having his first feed.

Harry Burnett smiled at the tender scene. Suddenly he felt like an intruder. 'You don't need me any more,' he said. 'I'll be on my way.'

The midwife, too, took the hint, sensing that it was a precious moment between the new parents. When they were alone, Anna looked up from her son and smiled at her husband.

'Happy?' she asked.

'Ecstatic!' he replied, with a lump in his throat.

They were upstairs in the huge bedroom that had been temporarily turned into a delivery room. The silken sheets and counterpane had been replaced by hospital-type cotton, but the ornate décor of the walls and carpet remained. Anna had felt, at first, that she would never get used to the luxury of the big colonial-style residence on the hill. Sir Lawrence had begged them to live with him, pointing out that they could have a whole wing to themselves. They wouldn't even know that he and Coral were there, except when they all wanted to meet up for dinner or a drink. But the main reason was that he was planning to return to the UK, and he wanted to ensure that the Sinclair dynasty carried on in Penasing.

And the first few months here have been wonderful! Anna thought blissfully. Simon had concentrated on finalising the surgical unit at the hospital leaving his young deputy from Singapore to carry out most of the work on the islands. This meant that he could spend more time with Anna, and as her expected date of confinement drew near, she had been more than grateful to him. But now that the baby was here she was going to encourage him to visit the islanders again, to supervise and extend the medical facilities there. In fact, she was hoping he would take her and their son occasionally!

And she would go down to Singapore to see Safiah again, she told herself. The old matriarch had mellowed during the few months she had been undergoing psychiatric treatment, and she loved living with Razali and his new bride in their smart apartment. She studiously maintained that the wonderful Dr Sinclair had performed a miracle on her legs, and everyone was happy to go along with the story. Anna had visited her a month ago and found her to be a new person. They had been able to chat together, woman to woman, for the first time. Safiah had wanted to tell her about the day Ibrahim died.

Apparently he had taken his mother to see a plot of land, where he proposed to have two small houses built—one for Safiah and one for Anna and himself. He had tried to persuade his mother to agree to sell her house, but she had refused. She told Anna that she now regretted this, because Ibrahim had been so angry with her as he drove back through the jungle.

Anna had patted her hand, insisting that she mustn't have regrets. It was all in the past and life must go on. The present was very good, and they could look forward to a happy future.

She had also found Coral to be very friendly, now that she was happily married to Sir Lawrence. During one of their chats Anna had been surprised to learn that it was Simon who was funding th

slands project from a medical trust fund set up by
is grandfather. Apparently the senior Sinclair
ad wanted his son Lawrence to become a doctor
ind had been disappointed when he entered the
Colonial Service. He was pleased with the philan-
hropic works and the consequent knighthood, but
ie still wanted a doctor in the family. When Simon
vas born, he set up the fund for his medical educa-
ion and any medical projects he might pursue.

He would have been so proud of his surgeon
grandson, Anna thought lovingly . . . and his great-
grandson too. She looked down at her son. The
baby had stopped sucking and closed his mouth
obstinately. Just like his father! she thought as she
saw the determined set of the tiny features. Gently
she removed him from her breast and handed him
o Simon.

'Put him in his cot, darling,' she whispered
gently. 'He can be bathed later. I want you to hold
ne.'

'It's a long time since I was able to get my arms
around you,' he said, tucking the tiny mite into the
bedside cradle. 'I thought I'd married an elephant!'

'You do exaggerate!' she laughed, as he took her
n his arms.

'But you love me just the same, don't you?'

She gave a sigh of contentment and snuggled up
o him. 'If you promise not to let it go to your head,
hen yes, I'll admit that I think you're the most
wonderful man in the whole world.'

'Don't overdo it!' He kissed her gently on the lips
and felt her loving response.

'And before long, we'll give Simon junior a little
sister,' he said softly.

'Why not?' came her muffled reply.

Mills & Boon

YOU'RE INVITED TO ACCEPT 4 DOCTOR NURSE ROMANCES AND A TOTE BAG FREE!

Doctor Nurse

Acceptance card

| NO STAMP NEEDED | Post to: Reader Service, FREEPOST, P.O. Box 236, Croydon, Surrey. CR9 9EL |

Please note readers in Southern Africa write to:
Independant Book Services P.T.Y., Postbag X3010, Randburg 2125, S. Africa

YES! Please send me 4 free Doctor Nurse Romances and my free tote bag – and reserve a Reader Service Subscription for me. If I decide to subscribe I shall receive 6 new Doctor Nurse Romances every other month as soon as they come off the presses for £6.60 together with a FREE newsletter including information on top authors and special offers, exclusively for Reader Service subscribers. There are no postage and packing charges, and I understand I may cancel or suspend my subscription at any time. If I decide not to subscribe I shall write to you within 10 days. Even if I decide not to subscribe the 4 free novels and the tote bag are mine to keep forever. I am over 18 years of age   EP23D

NAME _____

(CAPITALS PLEASE)

ADDRESS _____

_____

_____ POSTCODE _____

The right is reserved to refuse application and change the terms of this offer. You may be mailed with other offers as a result of this application. Offer expires March 31st 1988 and is limited to one per household.
Offer applies in UK and Eire only. Overseas send for details.

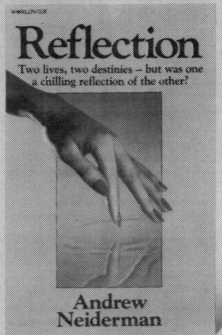